S0-BTZ-161

DARK TERROR

She awoke with a start.

Darkness was everywhere. It was probably the middle of the night. So why was she awake?

Then she heard the noise. The sound she had heard the night before—the flapping of wings. Where was it coming from? The hallway? The attic?

As quietly as possible, she slid out of bed and moved across the room. She listened. No more sounds. Holding her breath, she opened the door and, in the darkness, made her way down the stairs. Suddenly the sound seemed everywhere. The flapping of wings grew closer . . . louder . . . more furious.

She ran for the front door and out into the darkness. As she looked back at the house, she caught a movement in one of the windows . . .

A face was looking out at her.

Avon Books are available at special quantity discounts for bulk purchases for sales promotions, premiums, fund raising or educational use. Special books, or book excerpts, can also be created to fit specific needs.

For details write or telephone the office of the Director of Special Markets, Avon Books, Dept. FP, 1350 Avenue of the Americas, New York, New York 10019, 1-800-238-0658.

EDMUND PLANTE

If you purchased this book without a cover, you should be aware that this book is stolen property. It was reported as "unsold and destroyed" to the publisher, and neither the author nor the publisher has received any payment for this "stripped book."

ALONE IN THE HOUSE is an original publication of Avon Books. This work has never before appeared in book form.

AVON BOOKS
A division of
The Hearst Corporation
1350 Avenue of the Americas
New York, New York 10019

Copyright © 1991 by Edmund Plante
Cover art by Mark Fresh
Published by arrangement with the author
Library of Congress Catalog Card Number: 91-92045
ISBN: 0-380-76424-5
RL: 5.4

All rights reserved, which includes the right to reproduce this book or portions thereof in any form whatsoever except as provided by the U.S. Copyright Law. For information address Ruth Cohen Literary Agency, P.O. Box 7626, Menlo Park, California 94025.

First Avon Flare Printing: October 1991

AVON FLARE TRADEMARK REG. U.S. PAT. OFF. AND IN OTHER COUNTRIES, MARCA REGISTRADA, HECHO EN CANADA.

Printed in Canada

UNV 10 9 8 7 6 5 4 3 2

To my daughters, Jenny and Becky,
for encouraging me to write for young adults

Chapter One

"You have the house?" Cindy asked incredulously.

Joanne groaned inwardly, knowing what was coming next. She seriously thought of making up a lie, but her mind drew a blank. Besides, she could never pull it off. Cindy was too clever; nothing ever got past her.

"You *do* have the house!" Cindy squealed.

"I don't know when my parents will be back," Joanne said, hoping this would discourage her.

"Where did they go?"

Joanne was reluctant to answer.

"Come on, you can tell me."

"They went to Hawaii to celebrate their twentieth anniversary."

"How long will they be gone?"

"I don't know."

"Yes, you do. How long?" Cindy insisted.

"Two weeks."

"We can throw a party, Jo!"

It was exactly as Joanne had predicted, exactly as she dreaded.

"No, Cindy, no party. Not at my house."

"Why not?" Cindy looked around the living room, her short red hair hitting her cheeks as she turned her head in excitement, her brown eyes widening in approval as she took in the spacious surroundings. "It's perfect! An opportunity like this only comes once in a lifetime."

"Don't be silly."

"I'm not. I couldn't be more serious, Jo. Here's your big chance to make something of yourself! This is your chance to get Charlotte and Jerry and Missy and all the other popular kids to notice you. If you throw a party, they'll all finally know you're alive, and that—"

"You're exaggerating, Cindy. Besides, I don't care if they know I'm alive or not."

"That's not true."

Joanne opened her mouth to dispute this, but the expression on her friend's face stopped her. Belonging to the popular crowd meant a lot to sixteen-year-old Cindy. It had been equally important to Joanne, also sixteen, until she started dating Cliff Wright. Now she didn't care about Charlotte, Jerry, Missy, and any of the other popular kids anymore. She only cared about Cliff. With Cindy, unfortunately, it was different. She didn't have a boyfriend, so it still mattered that she wasn't accepted by the in crowd.

"It'll only be for one night," Cindy pleaded. "It'd be a night that could change our lives."

"Oh, brother, Cindy. Being a part of the group isn't all that important. We have each other. That's what's important."

"You have Cliff," Cindy reminded her. "Who do I have?"

Joanne sighed. "Oh, Cindy, I don't know about this party. I really don't want a bunch of kids here drinking and—"

"There'll be no drinking. None at all."

"There'll be a mess—"

"I'll clean it up. I promise."

"Well . . ."

"Please, Jo. Please!"

"If anything breaks, you're going to have to pay for it."

Cindy's eyes lit up as she realized Joanne was relenting. "You bet! I'll work double time, even triple time at the Pizza Hut to pay for whatever breaks—not that anything will, of course. Is it definite now? I'll call up some of the kids."

"I . . . I suppose it is. Mom and Dad never did say I couldn't have a party. They just said I shouldn't have Cliff here alone."

"There you go! You can have him here and you wouldn't be alone. You'll have a whole house full of people."

She ran to the phone.

"Cindy."

"What?" She had already dialed a number and was waiting for the phone to ring on the other end.

"Are you sure this is a good idea?"

"I'm positive. Stop worrying so much. We'll be careful. We'll make sure nothing gets out of control. You'll see. We'll have the best party anyone in Lemore High ever had!"

Four hours later, Joanne's house was filled with people chattering, laughing, and dancing. The stereo blared. Twice Joanne turned it down, fearing the neighbors would complain. After a while, she began to panic. She couldn't watch everybody at once. What if someone should accidentally knock her mother's favorite Tiffany lamp off the top of the TV? What if someone should spill soda on the blue carpet? What if someone should burn a hole in the couch with a cigarette?

Oh, why had she agreed to this party? She should have her head examined!

"Hey, relax," Cliff urged as he massaged her shoulders.

"I'm so afraid somebody's going to break or ruin something."

"The party's pretty tame. You've nothing to worry about."

He kissed her cheek, and for a moment she felt better. Maybe she was worrying needlessly.

She let Cliff pull her into his arms. His blue-gray eyes searched her face, patiently urging her to relax. His blond hair needed a trim, but then she liked his hair shaggy. It made him so cute, cuddly. She was so lucky.

She remained in his arms for a long while, blocking out her surroundings. Then she grew uneasy again. What if someone should break her father's favorite chair? Right now, two boys were sitting in it, and a third was perched on its arm.

Breaking away from Cliff, she hurried to the chair. "Please, only one at a time. My father'll kill me if you break it."

"We're only sitting on it," Peter Getty protested. He was the captain of the football team and wasn't used to having anyone tell him what to do.

"Too many are on it. Please get off."

Cliff joined her side. "You heard her. Get off."

Peter scowled at them, then finally complied. His two friends followed.

Joanne blew out a long breath. "Cindy thought this party would help us become more popular, but I think it's going to do the opposite."

"You threw this party to be popular?"

"No, I threw the party for Cindy. She wanted it badly, and I just didn't have the heart to refuse. I don't care about being in that crowd anymore. It seems so silly now."

"Speaking of Cindy," Cliff said, "there she is now."

Cindy was heading toward them. At five-feet-one, she could barely be seen threading her way through the crowd. "Hi! Great party, huh?"

"I suppose," Joanne said. "I didn't expect it to be this big. Did you call all these kids? There are some here I've never seen before."

"Yeah, I know. I think word got around that a great party was in progress."

"What?" Joanne couldn't believe what she was hearing. She began to count the strangers. There were at least six of them, mostly boys. "Some crashed the party?"

"Well, not really. Some of them asked to be invited, even pleaded, so I let them in. Why not? I thought it'd be less trouble to let them in," Cindy explained, seeing the frown on Joanne's face.

"But they're strangers, Cindy. We don't know them."

"They seemed okay. I made sure they didn't have any liquor on them. One of them is really cute, Jo."

Joanne groaned. Now she wished she had answered the door herself, instead of rushing about the house, making sure everything was safe or in its rightful place.

"You're not mad at me, are you?" Cindy asked.

"No . . . No, I guess not."

"Great. Tell you what. We won't let anybody else in. The party's big enough. Come on, let's go in the kitchen and make some more popcorn."

"I'll help," Cliff offered.

The kitchen was as crowded as the living room. Joanne, Cindy, and Cliff moved sideways to reach the cabinets and the stove.

As Joanne heated oil in a saucepan, she overheard some girls talking.

"What kind of monster?" a cheerleader named Charlene was asking Linda, another cheerleader.

"A zombie, a living dead man. Something like that," Linda replied. "They found him walking in the woods, not too far from here."

"Maybe he was on drugs."

"That's what Joey Watkins thought, but . . ."

"But what?"

"Well, Joey followed him. He said he was curious, said it was strange the way he was walking. It was almost as if he were floating in slow motion, not quite touching the ground. Joey kept his distance behind him, wondering where he was going. Then something distracted Joey, and he looked away for a second. When he looked back . . ." Linda paused, then lowered her voice ". . . the weird stranger was gone. He had vanished."

"Maybe Joey was the one on drugs," Charlene laughed.

"That's not true, and you know it. Anyway, he said this guy really spooked him, and he said if the guy had kept on going, he'd probably have come right straight to this place."

"Hey, maybe the guy, zombie, or whatever he is, heard about this party!" Charlene joked. "Maybe he's among us right now!"

Joanne felt a chill. A zombie among us? Right in this very house?

"You're burning the oil," Cindy said, nudging her.

"What?"

"The oil. You're going to have to start over."

The conversation between the two cheerleaders came to an abrupt halt as they looked over at Joanne.

Joanne stared dumbly at the saucepan. It was quickly filling with smoke. Cliff came to the rescue and took the pan away from her, covering it with a lid and smothering what could have been a fire.

"Y–you make the popcorn," Joanne told Cindy. Her hands were now shaking and her head was beginning to pound. She needed to be alone for a few minutes.

Without waiting for a response, she headed for her room. When she was at last alone, she tried to calm herself. In here the sounds from the party were muted. She wasn't certain why, but she was upset; her hands were still trembling. Having this party was definitely a mistake, she thought. She should have never let Cindy talk her into this.

Oh, why had she let her?

She knew it was because she was too soft. She was always afraid of offending people, afraid people wouldn't like her. As a little girl, she had foolishly given away her lunch money, even some of her toys, so that people would like her.

A knock sounded at the door.

"Jo?" Cliff called. "Are you all right?"

"Yes. Just a few more minutes. Okay?"

He hesitated a beat, then said, "Sure. I'll be waiting for you downstairs."

When he was gone, Joanne took in a deep breath. Never again, she vowed. She'd be grounded for a year if her parents ever found out about this.

As she forced herself to rejoin the party, she realized something else was bothering her. She couldn't pinpoint it at first, but an uneasy feeling was growing inside her, a feeling that wouldn't go away.

It bothered her that Cindy had allowed strangers into the house.

Chapter Two

The music blasted her ears the instant she opened her bedroom door. Someone had turned the stereo up again!

Covering her ears, Joanne ran down the stairs. The neighbors would definitely complain now. Also, the speakers on the stereo might blow.

As she reached the living room to shut off the music, she saw two boys shoving each other. "Oh, no," she groaned. "Please, no fights."

She pushed her way through the crowd toward the boys.

"Stop it!" she ordered.

They paid no heed to her. They were still shoving, each defying the other to swing first.

Frantically, Joanne looked around for Cliff. When she finally found him in another part of the room, she shouted his name. The music drowned her voice. She shouted again, this time succeeding in getting his attention.

"Tell them to stop fighting," she said when he reached her. "They won't listen to me."

Cliff went over to the boys, wrapped an arm around each boy's shoulder, and spoke calmly to them. To Joanne's relief, they listened and separated.

Deciding she'd had enough, Joanne worked her way toward the stereo and turned it off. Groans and protests punctuated the sudden silence. Heads pivoted toward her.

"Party's over!" she yelled for everyone to hear. "I want everybody out."

"What are you *doing*?" Cindy was suddenly beside her. "You can't throw everybody out like this!"

"I can, and I am."

"But . . . but it'll ruin you. It'll ruin us!"

"Don't be silly. I'm not going to have my house leveled just so we can be . . . liked."

"Now you're the one being silly. Nobody's doing anything to the house—"

Joanne left her and headed for the front door. She was confident now she'd made a mistake in throwing this party. Now, if it wasn't already too late, she was going to correct the mistake.

She flung open the door.

"You heard me, everybody! The party's over! Good night!"

Cindy rolled her eyes heavenward.

Cliff looked confused. "Why the sudden change of mind?" he asked Joanne.

"Because the music is too loud and the neighbors might complain. Because my house might get wrecked. Because a fight might break out. Because there are too many people in here, some of them strangers. Because—"

"Okay, okay!" He held up both palms. He turned to the crowd and helped Joanne shepherd them toward the front door.

When the house was empty, Joanne felt as though a hurricane had come and gone. The rooms certainly looked as if a storm had indeed hit. Paper cups, crushed pretzels and potato chips, and globs of clam dip littered the floors. In the middle of the living room, Cindy stood in a stunned state. It was not because of the house's horrible condition, Joanne knew, but because the party had ended abruptly, without warning.

"What—what—?"

Joanne turned to Cliff. "You have to go, too," she said. "My parents specifically forbade me to be alone with you in the house while they're away."

"That's not fair. What have I done for them not to like me?"

"They like you, Cliff. Really they do. It's just that . . . well, they're parents. They think we're babies, we can't behave ourselves." She looked at her surroundings again and added ruefully, "Sometimes they're right."

Cliff kissed her, then reluctantly left.

"I don't believe this," Cindy moaned, still in a daze. "My life . . . is over."

"No, it's not. Come on, help me clean up."

Joanne picked up the paper cups and dumped them in a wastebasket under the kitchen sink.

Cindy watched her for a long moment, then sighed miserably. "We'll be the talk of the school, and it won't be good. Everybody'll stay away from us as if we're a terrible disease." She pulled the vacuum cleaner out of a broom closet. "We might as well move to another town, maybe to another country."

Joanne tried not to laugh. "Don't you think you're exaggerating a bit?"

"Exaggerating? We're going to be the laughingstock of Lemore High, Jo! We'll never be able to show our faces again—"

"Cindy, it's not the end of the world. Even if the party were a huge success, it really wouldn't have changed anything. All those kids wouldn't have become our friends. Haven't you ever heard of the saying, 'He who has many friends has no friends?' It's better to have one true friend than a bunch of phony ones."

"What are you trying to say?" Cindy asked, frowning.

"I'm saying *I'm* your true friend. I would think that's more important than being popular with all those other kids. I know you mean more to me than all of them."

Cindy's face colored, and a smile slowly spread across it. "I guess you're right."

"I know I am. Now get to work!" Joanne barked. The two girls grinned at each other.

When the house was clean again, it was 10:30.

Neither girl was tired. They made tuna sandwiches and watched television.

"I'm sorry," Cindy blurted out during a commercial break.

"What?"

"I was a dope. I talked you into throwing a party, and it was selfish of me. Now you might get in a lot of trouble. Your parents will find out—parents always do, somehow—and it'll be all my fault. Promise me you'll tell them it was all my fault, Jo."

"Don't worry about it."

"What are you going to tell them?"

"The truth, that I had a party and regretted it."

They fell silent as a television program came back on. It was a comedy, but Joanne couldn't concentrate on it. Her mind was on her parents. Should she tell them about the party the minute they return from their trip, or should she forget about it and hope the neighbors never say anything? Oh, why had she done such a stupid thing?

"Jo, did you hear that?"

"Hear what?"

"A noise, upstairs."

Simultaneously, they looked up at the ceiling. Canned laughter exploded from the TV set.

"I didn't hear anything up there," Joanne said.

With the remote control, Cindy shut the TV off. Silence cushioned them.

"You must've heard something from the TV show," Joanne said.

"Shh. Listen."

They waited. Outside, a car went by, a dog barked. Inside . . . nothing.

"Put the TV back on," Joanne said. She refused to let Cindy frighten her.

Cindy, however, still had her ear angled toward the ceiling.

"Oh, stop it!" Joanne demanded.

"Something's up there, Jo. I swear."

"We're alone. Everybody's gone."

"How do you know that for sure?"

Cindy was right. How did she know? She hadn't counted heads . . . and the strangers Cindy had allowed into the house . . . had she seen them all leave?

"Turn the TV back on," Joanne ordered. She didn't want to think about it anymore.

Not hearing her, Cindy left the sofa and paused at the foot of the stairs. She looked up into the darkness, then at Joanne. "I have an awful feeling we're not alone."

Goosebumps sprouted on Joanne's arms, chilling her. She reminded herself that Cindy had a tendency to overreact. Nobody was upstairs. She and Cindy were the only ones in the house, and she told Cindy so.

"Maybe you're wrong," Cindy said. "Maybe everyone hasn't left."

"Look, Cindy, if you don't stop trying to scare me—"

"Shh!" Cindy interrupted again.

This time Joanne heard a noise. It was faint, the sound of footsteps on hardwood floor.

"Who . . . who do you think . . . ?" She couldn't finish.

Cindy lifted a finger to her lips. "I'll go see who's up there," she whispered.

"No!"

"I'm sure it's just one of the kids playing a prank on us."

"No, you're *not* sure."

"Well, what else could it be, the boogeyman?"

It could be any one of the strangers you had let in, she wanted to shout in reply. It could be somebody who is dangerous, or crazy! "I'll call the cops," she said.

"And get us in more trouble? No, that's a bad idea." Cindy glanced around the room until she spotted the set of brass implements beside the fireplace. Taking a heavy poker, she then climbed the stairs to the second floor. Joanne hesitantly followed.

"Be careful."

Halfway up the stairs they stopped.

Another sound reached them. It was different this time, not footsteps but a soft, fluttering noise. Maybe a bird was trapped inside the house. Maybe it wasn't a person at all.

"I bet somebody left a window open," Cindy said, apparently thinking of the same thing. "A robin or blackbird flew in and can't get out."

Convinced, the girls quickened their pace and reached the landing. They looked down one end of the short hallway, then the other. Nothing was out of the ordinary; no person waited for them; no bird flapped above them.

They checked Joanne's bedroom, flooding the room with light. Again, nothing was out of the ordinary. Cindy even looked under the beds and examined the closet. When they were sure nobody or nothing was in here, they searched in the master bedroom.

"Maybe it was only the wind hitting a window," Cindy said.

"Maybe."

Yet, to be sure, they inspected the bathroom, looked behind the shower curtain and inside the linen closet.

"How about the attic?" Cindy asked.

They looked up at the trap door in the ceiling. It was usually dusty up there. Cobwebs filmed the walls, and it was where spiders and, sometimes, mice lived.

"Maybe that's what we heard—mice," Joanne said.

"Do you want to check it?"

"No. It's creepy up there. Come on, let's go back downstairs. It's probably nothing we heard."

When they were back in the living room, watching TV, they heard the noise again.

It came from upstairs, as before. First they heard the flapping sound of wings, then they heard the footsteps.

The girls looked up at the sound.

It was directly above them.

Chapter Three

"Wake up," Cindy said, shaking Joanne. "Wake up."

Joanne opened her eyes to a slit. Bright morning light filled them. She closed her eyes again, then, yawning, reopened them.

It was a new day, and she was on the living room sofa. Groggily, she looked at her friend. Had last night been a dream? Had there really been a party?

Cindy nodded, sensing her thoughts.

Joanne groaned. "I'm doomed, doomed, *doomed.* I might be grounded until I'm twenty-one."

"We've been through that already. I wonder what those funny noises we heard last night were."

Now that she was completely awake, Joanne remembered them. After they had come downstairs, the girls had sat close together on the sofa, afraid. They had turned up the volume on the TV set to drown out any other sounds from upstairs. The last time Joanne remembered looking at the clock, it was ten after midnight. She must have fallen asleep shortly after that.

"Today's Saturday," Cindy said. "Let's eat out for breakfast, then go to the mall."

The suggestion was appealing. Joanne took a quick shower while Cindy waited in the living room.

"Don't you want to take a shower?" Joanne asked after she was done.

"Nah. I'll take one at home, later. Are you ready now?"

"Nobody's going to come after you with a knife while you're in the shower," Joanne assured her, grinning. "There'll be no bloody shower scene as you see in horror movies."

"I know that. I just don't feel like it, that's all. Let me just call my mom and let her know where we'll be, then we can go."

"Suit yourself, be dirty and smelly."

They ate a late breakfast and then went on to the South Lemore Mall. They tried on clothes and jewelry, sprayed each other with sample perfume from a cosmetic counter, and looked at CDs at a music shop. The girls ate lunch and then went to a movie at the mall theater.

"Hey, don't you have a date with Cliff tonight?" Cindy whispered around a mouthful of popcorn. A love scene on the huge screen had made her think of Joanne's boyfriend.

"He has tickets to a ball game. He knows I don't care for the sport."

"You let him go?" Cindy sounded surprised.

"Sure. Why wouldn't I?"

"Well, because it's Saturday night and he's your boyfriend."

"That doesn't mean we have to smother each other. I don't mind at all. It's good to have a Saturday night away from each other now and then."

"I guess. Hey, how would I know?" Cindy shrugged. "I don't have a boyfriend."

"You will, you will."

When they left the theater, the sun had sunk behind the building and the horizon was vivid with purple and pink clouds. A strong sense of dread filled Joanne, a sense that she repeatedly told herself was groundless and silly. Yet she was reluctant to go home.

"What do you want to do now?"

"I don't know. Maybe we could watch TV at my house. Maybe something good is on."

They spent the evening at Cindy's, watching a cartoon movie that her six-year-old sister, Hannah, wanted to see. Tomorrow was Hannah's birthday and she was permitted to stay up until ten o'clock to watch the movie.

When it was over, Joanne said to Cindy, "Will you sleep over at my house again tonight?"

She wasn't certain, but she thought she'd seen a flash of alarm in her friend's eyes.

"Gee, I don't think I can," Cindy replied, pulling a regretful face. "Hannah's having a birthday party tomorrow, and I promised to help Mom clean the house."

"You can still help her."

"I have to get up early."

"So you get up early at my house."

"Oh, I don't know," Cindy said. Her eyes darted everywhere, avoiding Joanne.

"It's only a five-minute drive to here," Joanne reminded her.

"I know, I know. But I don't think Mom will understand."

"Go ask her."

Cindy hesitated for a moment, then shook her head. "I don't think this will be a good time to ask."

"Why not?"

"Because it's at the last minute. She has this thing about asking for something at the last minute. Say, maybe you can sleep here, instead."

She left the room to talk to her mother, who was in the kitchen preparing a cake for Hannah. When Cindy returned, Joanne could tell by her friend's face that she'd been refused.

"If it were any other time, Mom would let you stay over," Cindy explained. "But she has so much to do, and she wants to get to bed early."

"We won't bother her."

"Oh, you know how mothers are. They can't sleep unless we're all safely tucked away in our beds."

"Then we'll be tucked away."

"She'd never believe us. She thinks we'd stay up late talking or watching TV."

"Tell her we'll go to bed the same time as she does."

"I know my mother, Jo. When she says no, it's no. It'll have to be some other time."

Joanne felt an icy sensation deep inside her stomach. She tried to ignore it, tell herself it was nothing, but the feeling wouldn't leave her. She stared silently at the TV.

"Are you okay, Jo?"

"Huh? Oh sure. Why wouldn't I be?"

"You're awfully quiet all of a sudden."

"Oh. No, I'm okay," Joanne assured her.

The sweet, warm smell of a cake baking in the oven permeated her nostrils. It was a cozy, *safe* aroma. Now, more than ever, she wanted to stay.

"Please," Joanne implored. She felt as if she were a little kid begging this way, yet she couldn't stop herself. "Ask your mother again."

Cindy sighed, then returned to the kitchen. This time her mother followed her back out to living room.

Now Joanne really felt foolish. Where on earth was her pride?

"I'm sorry, Joanne," Cindy's mother said gently, while wiping her hands on a dishtowel. "This really isn't a good time to sleep over. How about tomorrow night? I think that would be much better for all of us."

"No, I want to stay here tonight, Mrs. Harris."

Her own frank boldness shocked Joanne as well as Mrs. Harris.

"Why is tonight so important?" Cindy's mother frowned.

"I—I don't know. I didn't mean to be rude, Mrs. Harris. I'm sorry. I guess I'd better leave now."

"She'd be alone in the house, Mom," Cindy explained. "Her parents are away on vacation for two weeks."

"Oh. Is that why?" Mrs. Harris asked, looking intently at Joanne. "Are you afraid to be alone, dear? Well, if that's the case, then I guess I should let you stay here."

"No, never mind, Mrs. Harris. It's okay, really. I told my parents I was old enough to stay home by myself, and I am." She managed a smile and jumped to her feet. "Thanks anyway, Mrs. Harris. Good night."

"Are you sure?"

"Yes. I'll see you tomorrow, Cindy."

Cindy started to say something, then changed her mind. "Call me as soon as you get up."

Outside in her car, Joanne sat at the wheel for a long moment. What in the world was the matter with her? Mrs. Harris must think she was a big baby, a baby afraid to be alone.

Joanne sat in the Harris's driveway until she saw Mrs. Harris peek out the window. Quickly, Joanne turned the ignition and drove away. She rode around the neighborhood for awhile, not really caring she was wasting gas.

What was she afraid of? Was it of the noises she and Cindy had heard the previous night? They had checked the house, hadn't they? They hadn't found anybody or anything.

As she finally headed homeward, it occurred to

her that Cindy had probably lied. Was it really true that Cindy couldn't sleep over at Joanne's house because she needed to help her mother with the birthday party?

No, it was because she, too, was afraid.

Chapter Four

Joanne had never seen her house look so dark.

She stared at it from inside her car. The windows were black glass, revealing nothing within. She glanced at the houses on each side of hers; both were shadowy and silent. She hadn't really realized how late it was. She had spent a lot of time riding around in her car, and now it was probably well after midnight.

Steeling herself, she left the safety of the car and walked toward the front door. Her shoes clacked loudly on the flagstone walk. At the door, she fumbled in her pocketbook for the house key.

Before she unlocked the door, she pressed an ear against it. She heard nothing. She waited a minute more, just to be certain, and finally she went inside.

Immediately, Joanne reached for the wall switch

and turned on the foyer light. Her eyes rapidly took in the small room, each corner, and the arch that opened to the darkened living room. Nobody was in there.

And nobody was in the other rooms either, she told herself. There was nothing to fear. She was alone. She was safe.

She locked the door and latched the chain.

A sound caught her attention, paralyzing her. Somebody *was* here!

She grabbed the doorknob and pulled frantically, forgetting that she had just locked the door. She calmed herself when it occurred to her what the sound was—the faucet in the bathroom was dripping. In her rush to leave the house this morning, she must have failed to turn it completely off.

Relieved, Joanne switched the light off in the foyer, although not before turning on the light over the stairs. In the bathroom, she tightened the faucet until it stopped dripping. She felt a rush of guilt as she remembered that her father had warned her about this.

In her room, she closed the door. She considered tucking a chair under the knob. When am I going to get it through my thick skull that nobody is in the house with me? she thought.

She changed into an oversized nightshirt and climbed into bed. She turned off the lamp on the nightstand and closed her eyes, but her mind would not rest. Wind rattled the window. A dog barked far away. She turned over and covered her ears with the pillow.

Now the silence, as well as the darkness, was

too thick. Removing the pillow from around her ears, she reached for the lamp. She was too alert to sleep now.

She tried to read a Lois Duncan novel she'd started a couple of days ago. The book, *Summer of Fear*, was quite good, but scary. She quickly put the book aside. This was definitely not the appropriate time to read a story about a witch.

She scanned her small bookcase for something else to read. She had already read all the books on the shelves. Maybe there was something downstairs in the living room that she hadn't read yet—something that wouldn't frighten her.

Downstairs was too far away. Joanne didn't want to leave her room or the safety of her bed. There must be something she could do. Her gaze fell on her desk in the corner. Maybe she could do her homework, get it out of the way. Or maybe—

Without further thought, she reached for the phone and began dialing.

"Hello?" a groggy Cliff answered.

Joanne was grateful that Cliff had his own private line. Otherwise she'd have disturbed and possibly infuriated his parents.

"Cliff, did I wake you?"

"Yeah, you did. What time is it? What's wrong, Jo? Are you okay?"

"Oh nothing. I . . . just felt like talking to someone."

"But it's in the middle of the night!"

"So? There's no school tomorrow. You won't turn into a pumpkin."

She heard a faint, rustling sound on the other

end and knew Cliff was pulling himself upright in bed.

After a long pause, he said, "Something *is* wrong. What's the matter, Jo? Are you all right?" He yawned.

"Sure, I'm fine. How was the ball game?"

"Great. It was neck and neck all the way. But I don't think this is why you're calling me."

"Were there a lot of people at the stadium?"

"Yeah, it was packed."

"Did you have a good time?"

"I always do at the games. Come on, Jo, what gives? Why the small talk so late at night?"

"Nothing, really. It's just that I'm . . ." She bit back the word "scared" and said, "Lonely."

"You want me to come over?"

Joanne wanted to say yes, but she couldn't. She knew she was overreacting again, behaving like a baby afraid of the dark.

"Never mind, Cliff," she forced herself to say. "I should've never called."

"What do you mean, never mind?"

"I'll see you tomorrow."

"Hey, wait a minute—"

She hung up. Talking to him had made her feel a little better, although it had been foolish to call him. Now he knew the truth—she *was* a big baby.

Pulling the blanket up higher to her chin, she made another attempt to sleep.

The phone rang, startling her. Heart thundering within her chest, she grabbed the receiver.

She expected to hear Cliff's voice, but it was Cindy.

"I called to apologize." Her voice was low. Apparently, she didn't want her mother to overhear her.

"That's okay," Joanne said.

"My mother's been in a bad mood lately, and I was afraid to push it. Now I feel rotten about what I did. I should have insisted that Mom let you stay here tonight, especially after seeing how scared you were."

"I wasn't scared."

"Yes you were, and you still are."

"No, I'm not. Why would I be scared?"

"If you're not, then why was it so important you sleep over here tonight?"

"Because . . . because I was afraid I'd be bored."

"That's all?"

"Sure. Why on earth would I be afraid?"

"You know why. Because you're alone over there, and because last night we heard . . ."

Don't remind me! Joanne pleaded silently.

"Well, all I know is that *I* was," Cindy admitted, after a short pause. "So you're not mad at me, then?"

"Don't be silly."

"Well, I feel much better now. I'll see you later."

"No, wait!" Joanne said too loudly, too frantically. Swallowing, she willed herself to continue in a calmer voice. "Let's talk for a while. You wouldn't believe how bored I am here."

It was almost two o'clock when Cindy dropped

her voice and said, "Mom just knocked on the wall. That means I gotta hang up."

"Okay. Sorry for keeping you on the phone so long."

The phone clicked in Joanne's ear. The sound seemed so loud, so final.

She replaced the receiver, pounded her pillow into a more comfortable shape, and tried once more to fall asleep. The light shined in her face, making it impossible. She pulled the blanket up over her head. It was no use; the light penetrated the thin fabric, and she couldn't breathe very well under it.

There was no choice but to turn off the light.

As she finally drifted off to sleep, she heard the sound of fluttering wings. It came from the hallway, right outside her door. Or was it inside her room?

Only a dream, she reassured herself as she slipped into a deeper sleep. Only a dream.

Chapter Five

She awoke with a start.

She looked upward, looked to her right, then to her left. Darkness was everywhere. Where was she?

Gradually, she became aware of the mattress under her body and the pillow under her head. Now she knew she was in bed, in her room. It was probably the middle of the night. So why was she awake?

She recalled having a bad dream. She'd been running away from someone, someone who was a vague shadow. She ran through a maze, narrowly escaping the pursuer until she reached a dead end. The shadow had long arms, and when it extended them to enfold her, she opened her mouth to scream. That was when she woke up.

She'd been in darkness in her dream, and she

was in darkness now. Reaching for her lamp, she turned the light on. The alarm clock read 3:10. She groaned. It *was* the middle of the night.

The house seemed more quiet than usual. Shouldn't she at least hear the house settle or the refrigerator kick on? Was she more aware of the silence and stillness around her because she was alone?

She knew she'd never sleep now. The house seemed too big and the night too dark. Maybe she should wait for morning to come. It was only a few hours away.

As she pulled the covers closer to her chin, she began to recall more of her dream. When the shadowy stranger had cornered her in the maze, his feet had made loud, shuffling sounds. Had she only dreamt the noise? Or had she . . .

Crrreeeeak.

Her head swung toward the door. Had she really heard that?

She listened intently. Where had the noise come from—the hallway? The attic?

She heard it again. This time it was farther away, definitely from the hallway, but at the other end.

Joanne lay frozen with terror. Should she turn the light off and pretend she was still asleep? Or was it too late? Maybe the stranger had already seen the light from under the door. Maybe she should call someone. Call the police. Call Cliff.

Crrreeeeak.

Or maybe she should get out of the house.

She turned off the lamp, then waited a minute

longer to summon her courage. As quietly as possible, she slid out of bed, slipped into her robe, and moved toward the door. She listened. No more sounds came from the other side. Holding her breath, she opened the door.

She heard the sound again.

She started to slam the door shut, then caught herself. The sound had come from the other end of the house. Maybe the stranger was in her parent's room—and maybe the stranger was a burglar.

The sudden realization stopped her in her tracks. Her parents were being robbed, and here she was running away and letting the robbery take place. She should put a stop to this. After all, her parents had left her in charge of the house.

She should call the police. Yes, that's what she'd do. She'd sneak downstairs to the phone in the living room. The burglar might hear her if she used the phone in her own room.

In the darkness, she made her way down the stairs. When she reached the living room, she heard a new sound, a sound she had heard the night before—the flapping of wings.

She spun around. The sound seemed to be everywhere. She gripped the phone. With trembling fingers she began to dial.

"Hello, police! Police!"

"What's this, a prank?" a man grumbled from the other end. "Don't y'know what time it is?"

"Oh, I'm sorry. Wrong number."

Replacing the receiver, Joanne tried again.

The flapping sound grew closer. Not only was it louder but it sounded more furious, as though it came from something too big to be a bat or a bird.

Perhaps she should get out of the house now. She could call the police on another phone elsewhere.

As she ran out the front door, she heard the sound again, and knew the winged creature had begun to fly down the stairs. She slammed the door shut and bolted toward her car. It was locked.

Joanne fought back panic. She locked her car every night, and her keys were now in her room. She looked back at the house, debating whether or not to go inside for the keys. She caught a movement in one of the windows.

A face was looking out at her.

Joanne gasped. The face was ugly, its features distorted and blurry, as though pressing against the glass. It was difficult to see clearly, for only a half moon and a distant street lamp brightened the night.

She turned and fled. She didn't know where she was heading until she found herself three streets away, in front of Cliff's house. Hugging herself against the predawn chill, she looked up at her boyfriend's window. Of course it was dark, as was the rest of the house.

"Cliff," she called softly. "Cliff."

She knew he would never hear her. She'd have to raise her voice, and this would undoubtedly wake up the whole family. She thought of throwing pebbles against the window but couldn't find any in the dark night.

She sat on the porch. What could she do now?

Go back home and use the phone in there? Go to Cindy's house, which was another mile away? Or stay here and wait for daylight, wait for everybody to wake up?

Or should she try to wake everyone up herself?

No, that would be a bad idea, she told herself. This was her problem, and she shouldn't impose it on anyone else. Besides, she could be overreacting. Maybe she had only imagined the noise and the face in the window.

Leaning back against a post, she decided to wait. She closed her eyes and soon fell asleep.

"Joanne? Joanne, are you all right?"

She opened her eyes and was startled to find Cliff's mother looking down at her.

Joanne sat bolt upright as memory flooded back. Sunlight momentarily blinded her. "Oh, uh, I was locked out of my house, Mrs. Wright."

The excuse had been instinctive. Why couldn't she tell the truth? Was she embarrassed that she had rushed over here like a frightened child?

"How long have you been here?" Mrs. Wright asked.

"A few hours, I guess."

"You poor dear. You should've awakened us. We would've let you sleep inside."

"That's okay."

"No, it's definitely not okay. My, you must be absolutely frozen."

"I'm fine, Mrs. Wright. Really, I am."

"Well, you must come inside now. I'm making breakfast. Come on."

She helped Joanne to her feet, then opened the front door for her. She was insistent, leaving Joanne with no choice but to come into the house.

Cliff, bounding down the stairs, stopped short when he saw her.

"Jo, what—"

Suddenly aware she was wearing only a nightshirt and a cotton robe, she blushed. If only she could snap her fingers and magically disappear.

"I found her sleeping on our porch," his mother was saying, shaking her head incredulously. "Can you imagine? Don't you ever do anything like that again, Joanne. The next time you find yourself locked out of your house, you wake us up immediately. Do you understand?"

Joanne nodded.

"Good. Now, would you like one egg or two?"

When Mrs. Wright was gone, Cliff said, "Did you really lock yourself out?"

"Oh, Cliff." She fell into his arms and buried her face in his chest. "It was horrible! I've never been so scared in my life!"

"What happened?"

She told him about the strange sounds, the footsteps, and the flapping of wings. Then she told him about the face in the window.

"You think someone's inside the house?" he said.

"Yes. He's been in there since the party."

"Who, do you think?"

"I don't know. We let in so many strangers that night. I think someone came in and never left."

"Do you want to call the police?"

"I did last night, but I'm not so sure now. What if no one's there? The police will laugh at me. They might even call my parents. Everybody will think I'm a big baby. Maybe they're right—maybe I am too young to be left alone in the house. Maybe I should've stayed at my grandmother's. Or maybe I should've asked my parents to hire a baby-sitter—"

"Take it easy, Jo. You're being too hard on yourself. Come on, let's have breakfast. Afterwards, we'll go to your place." He kissed the top of her head.

She wished she could believe him, but she couldn't stop thinking about the face in the window. It hadn't even looked human.

Chapter Six

The house looked so different in the sunshine.

For a fleeting moment, Joanne wondered why she'd been afraid. She looked over at Cliff behind the wheel. He seemed to be thinking the same thing. How could anyone fear anything from this freshly painted white house with its pretty curtains in the windows and green welcome mat before its door?

"Come on," Cliff said, jumping out of his car.

No, there was nothing at all to fear. Yet Joanne moved with dread.

She glanced at the window where she'd seen the face the previous night.

"Was that where you saw him?" Cliff asked.

"Yes."

"Are you sure?"

Joanne looked at him. Was he doubting her now? Was he letting the sunshine fool him?

He reached the front door.

"Do you want me to go in alone?"

Joanne shook her head and followed him into the house. When nothing jumped out at them, she relaxed.

"Wait a minute, I just thought of something," Cliff said. "We're not supposed to be in here alone. Remember?"

"There's an exception to every rule, and this is certainly an exception."

The house was silent. It was a different kind of silence, though. Peaceful. Amber sunlight slanted through a small window, warming and brightening the foyer.

Joanne and Cliff listened for sounds.

"I don't think anybody's here," Cliff whispered.

"How do you know that? We haven't checked the whole house yet."

"But it's so quiet in here."

"That doesn't mean anything."

Cliff nodded, realizing she was right. He peeked into the kitchen, then went upstairs, Joanne close at his heels.

"What's this?"

Something was on the hallway floor. He picked it up, examined it briefly, then gave it to Joanne. It was a feather.

She turned it over in her hand. The feather was black and shiny, almost bluish.

"Looks like you were right about a bird being in here," Cliff said. "I wonder if it did any damage trying to get out. I heard birds can get nasty and violent when they can't find their way out of places."

He headed for the bathroom.

"Cliff, wait."

He was gone, already in the other room. Joanne studied the feather again. It was rather large. Where had it come from? Was it really a bird's? She let the feather drift to the floor and followed Cliff into the bathroom.

It was empty.

"Cliff?"

He didn't answer. She pushed the shower curtain back. He wasn't in there either, although she couldn't imagine why he would be. She looked out the window, and still she could find no trace of him. Where on earth had he gone? She was certain she'd seen him enter this room. So how could he have disappeared so quickly? There was no other door, only the window.

"Cliff, where are—"

A hand dropped on her shoulder. "Gotcha!"

She jumped. When she realized it was Cliff who had snuck up behind her, she whirled on him.

"Where were you?" she shouted.

"Hey, take it easy. I was behind the open door. I saw you look for me in the shower." He grinned.

"It's not funny, Clifford Wright!"

His grin faded as he saw how frightened and furious she was. He attempted to pull her into his arms, but she wrenched herself loose.

"I was only playing a little joke," he said.

"Well, I'm not in the mood for your jokes."

"Gee, Jo, what's wrong? I've never seen you this mad before."

"You know what's wrong. Somebody's been in here. Somebody who could *still* be in here."

"I thought we already decided it was only a bird."

"Where is the bird now?"

"I don't know. I came in here to see if it tried to break through the window. Maybe it went up the fireplace in the living room."

"The flue's closed."

"Are you sure?"

"Yes. No. I don't know. Anyway, you're forgetting something. I also heard footsteps. I saw a face in the window."

"Maybe it was the bird you saw."

Joanne shook her head positively. "It was a man's face. At least, I think it was a man's. Whatever it was, it was ugly—and it was definitely not a bird."

"Well then, how do you explain the feather?"

"I don't know. Maybe both a bird and a man were here."

"I'll check the other rooms," Cliff said, going back out into the hallway. "We'll get to the bottom of this."

Joanne followed him throughout the house. No more feathers were found, although a strange odor lingered in her parents' bedroom.

"I don't smell anything," Cliff said after Joanne had questioned it.

"You sure?" The smell was faint and elusive.

She moved to various parts of the room, attempting to catch another whiff.

"What does it smell like?"

"I'm not sure. It's not a good smell. It's—" The odor suddenly filled her nostrils, then as quickly was gone. She grimaced with distaste. "Stale urine, I guess."

"Really? Do you think somebody—"

"There's also another smell," she interrupted. "Sulphur."

"Sulphur?"

"Yes, something like the smell you get after you burn a match."

"Maybe the bird was smoking." Another grin spread across his face.

"Be serious, Cliff!"

He pulled her into his arms, and this time she didn't try to free herself. Instead, she leaned her head against his shoulder and fought back tears.

"I'm sorry," she heard Cliff say softly. "I'm being a real jerk, aren't I?"

She didn't answer, needing the moment to compose herself. She took in a deep breath, then disengaged herself from his arms.

"Let's get out of here."

"We haven't checked the whole house yet. We still have the cellar and attic left."

She shuddered at the thought of searching those dreary places. "No way, Cliff."

"We'll never know if anybody's here if we don't check."

"I'm not going in the cellar or attic," she said adamantly.

"Then I'll go. Do you have a flashlight?"

"It's in one of the kitchen drawers."

After he found the flashlight, he said, "I'll only be a sec." Joanne followed him to the cellar door.

"Maybe this isn't a good idea," she said.

"Stop worrying. I'll give the cellar a quick look, that's all."

As he went down the stairs, Joanne watched him and a tug-of-war raged inside her. She was too afraid to join him, yet she felt guilty remaining behind.

"Cliff, no!" she shouted when he reached the bottom. "Let's get out of here."

"But I'll only be a minute."

"No. Please don't argue, Cliff. Please come back up."

He frowned, glanced at the gloomy cellar, then back at Joanne. He joined her at the top of the stairs.

"I don't know what the big deal is," he said.

"Somebody could be down there."

"I can take care of myself."

"Don't be an idiot, Cliff. What if he has a gun?"

"Then I'll raise my hands and say 'Please, oh please, don't shoot!' " He said in a dramatic, pleading voice, then laughed and gave her a quick kiss.

She scowled at him. "Always joking, aren't you? Come on, let's leave."

"What about the attic?"

Ignoring the question, she headed for the front door, opened it, and waited for him to follow her.

He threw his arms up in mock exasperation, shook his head, and stepped outside.

When they were back at his house, Joanne began to feel foolish again. What was she going to do now? Her parents would not be back for almost two weeks.

"You still look upset," Cliff said, watching her.

Joanne tried to mask her feelings with a smile. "I'll be all right."

"Do you want to stay here until your parents get back?"

The invitation surprised her. It would solve her problem, wouldn't it? She wouldn't have to worry about being alone in that house.

"Are you sure your parents wouldn't mind?" she asked, remembering that Cindy's mother had flatly refused to let her stay the previous night.

"Nah. My sister's room hasn't been used since she got married. You could sleep in there."

Joanne wanted to hug him, to lavish kisses all over his face. "That'd be great, Cliff! Go ask your parents now."

Ten minutes later everything was all set. Cliff's mother and father could see no reason why Joanne couldn't spend the next two weeks with them. Joanne offered them money that she had earned as a nurse's aide at a nursing home, but they refused to take it. "You're our guest," Cliff's father insisted. "We'd love to have you stay with us."

That evening she played Scrabble with Cliff and his parents. The time passed swiftly and pleasantly. Not once did she think about her house and the mysterious sounds she'd heard or the distorted face she'd seen. It was behind her now, and it would stay that way until her own parents were back from their vacation.

But later, alone in Cliff's sister's room, she was tormented by guilt. She wondered what was happening at her house. Was someone in there? Was there really a bird loose inside? Would the stranger and the bird damage the house, now that she was away? Would they destroy it, somehow? Burn it down?

Before her parents had left for their anniversary trip, they had been uneasy about leaving her alone.

"Are you sure you don't mind, dear?" her mother had asked.

"You worry too much, Mom," she had replied. "What could possibly go wrong? I'm sixteen, you know. I'm not a baby anymore."

"I know, dear, I know. It's just that we never left you alone this way before. We can't help but worry."

"You've got nothing to worry about," Joanne assured her. "The house will be safe with me."

"Don't forget to lock the doors at night or when you're gone," her father had reminded her. "And remember to keep an eye on the bathroom faucet. It doesn't always shut off the way it should."

"I know all about that, Dad. Just go and have a good time. Don't worry about the house. I'll take care of everything. You can trust me," she had said.

Now her parents were away, fully trusting her with the house. And here she was, somewhere else, abandoning the house. She felt as if she were a traitor. She knew now she could never stay here for two weeks—not if she wanted to live with herself.

She would have to go back to her own house.

She glanced at a clock on the nightstand. It was too late to leave now. Cliff and his parents were sleeping, and she didn't want to disturb them. Tomorrow, she vowed, she'd start fresh. Tomorrow, she'd start behaving like a responsible young adult.

Tomorrow she'd go back to her house, where she belonged.

Chapter Seven

The next morning, she told Cliff she was going back home after school. He tried to talk her out of it.

"No, Cliff," she said adamantly. "I promised my parents I'd look after the house, and that's exactly what I'm going to do."

At school, shc busied herself with her studies so intently that she was surprised when she heard the last bell. The hours had flown by so quickly!

It was late afternoon when Cliff dropped her off at her house. Mrs. Pearl, Joanne's next door neighbor, called out to her as soon as Cliff drove away.

"Joanne, Joanne!" the woman cried, hurrying toward her. She was somewhere in her fifties and plump. The short run between her house and Joanne's had already tired her, left her breathing arduously.

"I'm so glad . . . so glad to have caught you," she gasped.

"What's wrong, Mrs. Pearl? You look awfully upset."

"I . . . I am. I just had to tell you what happened."

"Would you like to come in and sit down?"

"No, no. I've a million things to do. I've supper to make, laundry to the ceiling . . . No, no. I just want to tell you about last night. Now, I don't want to frighten you. No, no. That's the last thing in the world I would want. I just want to be sure you lock your doors and your windows."

"Why, what happened, Mrs. Pearl?"

"I had the most frightful experience, dear. I was in my bedroom, you see, and I heard the strangest sound outside the house. When I looked out my window, I had the shock of my life! Somebody was looking in at me! And, as you already must know, my bedroom is on the second floor. The man must have had a ladder."

"That's horrible, Mrs. Pearl! What happened next?"

"I screamed, of course. I grabbed something, I think it was a hairbrush. Not much of a weapon, I must admit, but it seemed to have discouraged the man, nevertheless. He disappeared. Then I called the police. It was dreadful. Dreadful."

"Did the police come?"

"Yes, but it was too late. They couldn't find anything, not even footprints outside the house."

"What did this man look like?" Joanne asked.

"Did you give the police a good description of him?"

"No," the woman said ruefully. "I couldn't see him too clearly. It was a dark night, remember, and it all happened so fast. He was there one minute, and then gone the next. I'm afraid the police didn't believe me."

"But you did definitely see a man in the window?"

"Oh, yes. I'm certain of it, dear. There's a prowler loose in the neighborhood. I know I'm scaring you, but I had to warn you. I just had to."

"I understand, and thanks, Mrs. Pearl."

"Please do be careful. Lock your doors and windows tonight. He could come back, you know." The woman solicitously patted Joanne's hand, then hurried back to her own house.

At the front door, Joanne hesitated. What had her neighbor really seen last night? Had it been the same stranger Joanne had seen looking out at her two nights ago? Was it the same horrible face?

Joanne looked over at Mrs. Pearl's house. It was a big house, partly hidden behind an overgrown maple tree. The second-story windows, she noted, were far from the ground. An intruder would definitely need a ladder to peek into one of those windows—a big ladder. It was difficult to picture a man carrying such a cumbersome object while stalking the neighborhood. And besides, Mrs. Pearl had never mentioned seeing a ladder. She had only assumed one had been used beneath her bedroom window.

So what did this mean? Had the prowler *flown* to the window? Of course not!

Inside her own house, Joanne locked the door, wondering if she was doing the right thing. What if the stranger was inside the house and she was locking him in? No, she firmly told herself, he's not in the house anymore. He had been roaming the neighborhood and was now probably somewhere across town, maybe even in another town.

Uneasy with the silence in the house, she turned on the television set. She glanced at a clock. It was 4:30. Late afternoon shadows dimmed the rooms, made them gloomy. She thought of checking the entire house, then changed her mind. She had searched the place both with Cindy and with Cliff, and had found no one.

She watched TV for awhile, losing herself completely to a program. When it was over, it was six o'clock, and shadows had thickened to darkness.

Quickly, she turned on a lamp. There's nothing, she reminded herself. She was alone in the house.

Nothing had happened so far, so why should she be afraid now, just because it was nighttime?

If somebody was still in the house, she'd have heard or seen him by now. Wouldn't she?

Suddenly hungry, she went into the kitchen and made herself a hamburger. As she ate it, she sensed a change in the room. She looked behind her. Everything was the same. She glanced out the window. As far as she could see, nobody was out there. Although the back door was already locked, she unlocked and locked it again.

Then she sat back down at the table to finish her hamburger.

Again she sensed a change in the room. She tried to define the feeling. Was it a presence she was feeling? Was it a thickness in the air, a drop in temperature?

Actually, it seemed to be all three. Someone, she was certain, was watching her. A strange mist seemed to be slowly developing in the room, at the same time chilling it.

All in her head, she told herself. Nothing has changed. She took another bite of her hamburger.

A rotten stench filled her nostrils. Was it the hamburger? She thought she'd cooked it thoroughly, but it was now dripping down her fingers, oily and pink. Grimacing, she put the hamburger back down on her plate.

Her stomach heaved. The stench grew stronger. She picked the hamburger up and threw it into the garbage disposal.

Still the nauseating odor lingered.

Where was it coming from? Now it seemed to be everywhere in the room. Also, the air seemed to be thickening even more, turning into a smoky mist. And the temperature was still dropping.

I'm dreaming, she thought. I must be!

The mist and stench began to fade. A deep, melodic voice spoke to her.

"Hello, Joanne."

She spun around.

Someone was standing in the doorway to the living room.

Chapter Eight

Joanne gasped.

The stranger smiled at her. It was a smile that was charming, yet chilling.

"At last we meet," he said, bowing slightly. He was a young man, somewhere in his twenties. Although he was handsome, with thick, ebony hair and soft, dark eyes, his skin was unnaturally pale and his lips were too red. When he parted his rather large mouth, his teeth gleamed somewhat yellow against the sickly pallor of his complexion.

Joanne took a step back. "Who are you?"

"You invited me. Remember?"

"No."

"It was a lovely party. I enjoyed it immensely."

"I—I don't know who you are, but I think you'd better leave right now!"

"Now, now, don't be afraid, my lovely one." He extended a hand, which she ignored. "If given a chance, we could get along famously."

"I'll call the police if you don't—"

The room began to dim. Or was she going to faint? The young man's face wavered as his dark eyes stared at her. She wanted to shout at him again to leave, but she could not find her voice.

The man moved closer.

"Yes, I think we could get along very well," she heard him say in that smooth, hypnotic voice.

Dully, she was aware that he was appraising her. His smile broadened. Then his mouth opened to bare his teeth, which now seemed different—sharper.

She wanted to run from this man, yet her legs would not comply. His face loomed closer, closer.

The phone rang.

Startled, Joanne jumped. When the phone rang a second time, the spell, or whatever it was that had entranced her so, shattered.

"Get out of here!" she screamed, stumbling away from him.

He glared at her, furious that he had failed. Then he threw his head back and laughed.

"Out of here!"

She ran for the phone. When she reached it, it stopped ringing. Snatching the receiver, she dialed for the police. Before she could finish, however, she heard a raucous caw behind her. She spun around and saw a black bird swooping forward.

She ran away from it, dropping the receiver.

The bird dived toward her, missed by mere

inches, then soared toward the ceiling. At length it alighted on the fireplace mantel, where it watched her with cold, flat eyes.

Joanne reached for the phone again, and once more the bird charged at her.

The bird was actually guarding the phone. She contemplated using the extension in her bedroom. She was near the stairway now; it would be easy.

She broke into a run up the steps. Moving faster than she'd ever moved in her life, she reached her room and slammed the door shut behind her. Then she listened, her ear pressed against the door. She couldn't believe it! She had actually escaped the bird!

She ran to the phone and, with trembling fingers, started dialing. This time she finished, but the phone at the other end would not stop ringing. Why were the police taking so long to answer?

In the periphery of her vision something moved. Turning her head, she saw the doorknob move! Oh, why hadn't she thought of locking it? Now it was too late!

"Hello, Lemore Police Department," a voice said over the phone.

"This is . . . is . . ." Her eyes riveted on the door, Joanne could barely speak.

"Hello? Hello?" the voice at the other end demanded.

The door opened. The handsome stranger was smiling coldly at her.

Joanne slammed the receiver down, then froze, not knowing where to go, what to do. The stranger entered the room. Joanne skirted the walls to keep her distance from him. When she saw that the door was wide open and empty, she made a dash for it.

She raced down the hall and down the stairs. As she glanced over her shoulder, she expected to see the stranger chasing her, but it was the bird she saw again. It flew past her, cawing stridently. She thought of using the living room phone, then changed her mind. It was useless. She should just get out of the house!

As she pulled at the door, she found it locked. Of course! She had locked it when she first came in!

"Why are you running away from me, lovely princess?"

She gasped. He was directly behind her now, both hands flat against the door, imprisoning her. How had he gotten down here so fast?

"Leave me alone!" she screamed.

"Please do not be afraid, my lovely one."

"Who are you?"

"I am your prince. You are my princess."

She could feel his breath on her neck. It was wintry, numbing. "Go . . . away," she pleaded.

"You are so lovely. Please don't run away from me."

Gently, he placed his hands on her shoulders and turned her to face him.

"So, so lovely," he whispered.

He lifted her hair off her neck.

She could feel herself losing consciousness.

"No!" she cried. With all the strength she could muster, she punched him in the stomach.

He grunted, more out of surprise than pain.

Frantically, she released the lock, flung open the door, and fled into the night.

Chapter Nine

She ran to a large elm at the edge of the front yard, then stopped. Under this tree she felt somewhat protected, knowing she was shrouded in shadow. She looked back at the house.

Yellow lights were on in the kitchen and living room. She half expected the young man to appear at one of the windows, to look for her. He didn't.

Everything had happened so fast. Now Joanne wasn't sure if any of it had been real. Where had the black bird come from? Did it belong to the young man? Had he brought it here? Or had it unwittingly flown in that night of the party and been trapped inside? Was it still searching frantically for an exit?

She shuddered as her thoughts returned to the stranger. He was handsome, yet he gave her the creeps. She hated how he had stared at her. His eyes and smile had been cold and, at the same time, spellbinding.

Had he actually hypnotized her?

Had he somehow caused her to imagine everything?

God, how had she ever gotten herself into this mess!

Joanne looked over at Mrs. Pearl's house. Perhaps she could call the police from there.

When she saw that all the windows were dark, however, she changed her mind. This was her problem, not Mrs. Pearl's. It would be unforgivable to wake the woman up and burden her with it.

Joanne considered returning to Cliff's house. His parents had made her feel so welcome. Yet . . .

It was not their problem either.

The key to her car was still in her room, once again leaving her with no transportation.

Frustrated and angry, she sat at the base of the tree. It was all so unfair that the young man was putting her through this—in her own house!

Somehow, she would have to make him—and his horrible bird—leave.

The lights in the kitchen and living room went out.

Now the house looked foreboding . . . dangerous.

Joanne stared at it, trying to muster up courage. She was still looking at it when her eyes began to grow heavy.

She felt braver when she woke up, although nothing seemed to have changed. Her short sleep had strengthened her resolve and weakened her fear. The young man was probably a vagabond, needing a temporary place to stay and eat. He had heard Joanne was alone and had decided to take advantage of her.

Well, she wasn't going to let him push her out of her own house anymore!

Inside, she flicked on lights and moved straight for the fireplace poker in the living room. Then, feeling a little more secure, she looked around. To her surprise she found a cat curled up on the sofa. It yawned and gazed lazily back at her.

Its fur was black and its eyes were golden—like the bird's.

"Go on! Scat!" Joanne threw open the front door and clapped loudly, hoping to scare the cat into leaving.

The animal calmly watched her without moving from its place on the sofa. Its eyes glittered as if it were delighted that Joanne had finally noticed it.

"Get out of here! *Git*!" Joanne prodded the animal with the poker. She wondered where the young man was. It drew back, spat at her, and leaped off the couch. But instead of going out the door, it sprinted up the stairs.

"No!" Joanne shouted, running after it. "Go outside! Get out of the house!"

When she reached the hallway at the top of the stairs, she couldn't find the cat anywhere. She was about to give up and go back downstairs when a movement in the periphery of her vision caught her attention. She pivoted and found the young man leaning against the doorway to her bedroom.

"I'm delighted you decided to return," he said, smiling. "What is that rod in your hand, lovely princess?"

Joanne gripped the fireplace poker tighter. "Who are you? What are you?"

"Me? Why, my name's Erik. It means 'ever powerful,' if you must know."

"What are you doing here?"

"I know your name," he went on, as if she'd never spoken. "And I know your friends call you Jo. It does not suit you. You're much too lovely to have such a crude nickname. Would you mind terribly if I call you princess, my lovely one? It is so much more fitting."

"I said, what are you doing here? You're trespassing on private property."

"You, or rather, one of your friends, invited me."

"That was for the party which, I shouldn't have to tell you, is over. Look, whoever you are—"

"I've already told you, I'm Erik. The name also means 'kingly.' " His smile broadened.

"Get out of here."

"But it's such a lovely house, princess."

"If you're not out of here by the count of three, I'll . . . I'll take drastic measures," she threatened, now clutching the poker with both hands.

He laughed, then as quickly grew serious. "I don't know why you're so afraid of me. Don't you like me?"

"I'm not afraid of you," she lied. "You're a

stranger. I don't know you, nor do I want to. My parents left me in charge here, and I can't let you stay. *Now get out!*"

"Yes, you are afraid. But please don't be. Don't you find me attractive? I find you attractive." He took a step closer. "Relax. We should permit ourselves to know one another. I think you will like me if we do. I am certain I will like you."

"I mean it. One . . . two . . ."

"Please do give me a chance . . . give yourself a chance."

He grew nearer. "Yes," he said approvingly in his deep, smooth voice, "give us both a chance." Joanne found herself unable to look away from him. Her hands on the poker trembled.

He stared at her, then gently stroked her cheek with a long finger. The touch was icy, startling her. Then it grew warm, even pleasant.

"I don't know if you're aware of this, but you are a beautiful young lady, princess," he said.

No one had ever called her beautiful before. Not even Cliff. Embarrassed, she looked away. Gently, he cupped her chin and turned her face back toward him.

"Please don't be shy, precious one."

He gazed longingly at her lips. He was going to kiss her! And what was more incredible was that she found herself wanting him to!

His face leaned forward. Quickly, she averted her head.

"I–I have a boyfriend," she stammered.

"Please do not think about him. Think only of

this moment, of how wonderful . . . yes, wonderful . . . this moment could be."

"No, I—"

"Please. Be free. Feel free."

As she felt herself drift, her hands clutched and unclutched the fireplace poker. Groggily, she wondered why she was holding it.

Then the spell, dream, or whatever it was, broke and she saw alarm flicker across his face. He was staring at something behind her. Puzzled, she turned to see what it was.

Down below in the foyer, morning light was filtering through the window. As far as she could see, nothing was unusual.

When Joanne looked back, Erik was gone.

Chapter Ten

She couldn't stop thinking about Erik.

The day was a hazy blur. It was Sunday, so she stayed home and slept on and off. Even her dreams were filled with the handsome stranger. Where had he come from? When would she see him again? What was wrong with her?

Vaguely, she remembered she'd been afraid of staying inside the house, but that seemed so silly now as she looked around at the empty rooms and the inanimate furniture. There was nothing to fear. The silence was peaceful, with golden sunlight pouring in through the windows. It was almost as if she'd drunk too much wine, for everything was so dreamy, making her smile as her heart swelled.

Erik.

She even liked the name. It suggested power and strength.

She had never felt this way before. Was it love? Her feelings for Cliff were not quite like this, not this strong, anyway, and certainly not this sudden. She felt as if she'd been shot with an arrow—Cupid's arrow.

The phone rang, startling her.

Erik?

Heart thundering, she grabbed the receiver. "Hello?"

"Hi. It's me, Cindy."

"Oh."

The disappointment was not lost on her friend. "You thought I was Cliff?"

"No. Somebody else."

"Who?"

"Erik."

"Who?"

Joanne rubbed her forehead in a subconscious attempt to clear her mind. Everything was fuzzy, and talking was becoming a difficult effort. She felt as if she were more asleep than awake.

"Hey, Jo, are you all right?"

"Sure. Why?"

"I don't know. I can barely hear you. And you're not saying much."

"No. I–I'm fine. I'm . . . I'm—"

"You're what?" Cindy prompted.

"In love."

"Say that again?"

"In love . . . I think . . . Really in love."

"With Cliff, you mean? Yeah, I know that. Everybody in Lemore High knows that."

"No . . . I already told you. Erik."

"What on earth are you talking about?" Cindy demanded after an incredulous pause. "Who is this Erik?"

"Well, he's the handsomest boy I've ever seen. I couldn't even begin to describe him, he's so gorgeous."

"When did you meet this guy? Where did you meet him?"

"Last night. I met him at . . . well, I'm not sure. I just remember being with him here. Everything's so hazy."

"I don't believe what I'm hearing! This is awfully sudden, don't you think?"

"But isn't that how real love is—sudden? Out of the blue? Love at first sight?" Joanne sighed dreamily. "It was like that, Cindy. He looked at me. I looked at him. And then . . ."

"What about Cliff?"

"What about him?" An image of Cliff floated into Joanne's mind, then quickly vanished as Erik's flawless face appeared in its place.

"The last time I saw you, it was Cliff you liked. Remember?" Cindy reminded her. "You've liked him for quite a while now. You two were—are—the perfect couple."

"I can hardly . . . remember what he . . . looks like anymore," Joanne whispered, speaking more to herself than to her friend.

"Hey, I bet you've been drinking! Have you?"

"No."

"You gotta be. You're not yourself at all."

Joanne sighed. "You don't understand. I'm in love. I never felt this way before."

"Do you want me to come over?"

"No. I think I'm going to take another nap. I'm really tired."

"Are you sure?" Cindy sounded worried. "I promised Mom I'd take Hannah to the movies and out for some ice cream. I guess I could always postpone it and—"

"Don't be silly. Like I said, I'm going to take a nap."

"Well, all right," Cindy said uncertainly. "I'll talk to you later—when you're sober."

Joanne decided to let it go. How could she explain it to her anyway, especially when she herself wasn't certain what was happening. She was pretty sure she hadn't had anything to drink. Yet she couldn't remember ever feeling so heady and euphoric. Maybe Cindy was right, maybe after a nap her head will be more sober.

When Joanne woke up, however, Erik was still on her mind, although not quite as vivid or as fresh.

"Hello, princess."

Joanne spun around on the couch. The voice had come from the foyer, from the top of the stairs.

"Erik?"

"The one and only."

She was surprised to find darkness all around her. Clicking on a nearby lamp, she glanced at the brass and glass anniversary clock on top of the fireplace mantel. It was 9:30! She had slept away the entire afternoon and part of the evening!

"I see you've been waiting for me," said Erik.

Feeling somewhat like a sleepwalker, she followed his voice to the stairs. He was on the top step, looking down at her, his long arms spread to welcome her, to enfold her. He looked so tall and so powerful up there.

"Come," he whispered. "I've waited all day."

"You missed me?" It surprised her that one so handsome would find her attractive.

"Oh, yes," he assured her. "Very much."

"Where were you today? I was hoping you'd be back sooner."

"I need my rest. Now we have the night free. Come. Please do not keep me waiting any longer. Come into my arms."

Joanne took another step, and he smiled, nodding—a little too eagerly, she noted.

She paused. Somewhere, deep inside her, there was cold uncertainty.

Why was she so attracted to this stranger? She scarcely knew him. Before this, she had taken pride in the fact that she'd never let herself be drawn to the popular, good-looking boys in school, that she had always peered beneath the surface of their handsome faces to find true depth.

It was how she had become attracted to Cliff. He was beautiful all the way through.

But Erik . . . she did not know him at all, yet she was falling so hard . . .

"What's wrong, princess?" He came downstairs toward her, keeping his arms extended.

"I—I'm sorry. I'm so confused. I feel as though I'm in some kind of trance. I've been this way all day."

"Confused about what? Certainly not about me?"

She nodded. "I don't even know you, Erik."

"Then by all means get to know me."

"You don't understand. This is all happening too fast. I feel as though I'm being pulled into some kind of whirlpool."

"Nonsense," Erik chuckled. He paused at the step directly before her and gently let a slender finger caress her cheek. "Why hold back, lovely one?" His voice was husky, yet soft. "Why not go, as they say, with the flow?"

His finger moved to her lips, outlined them.

"Look into my eyes." He whispered the command. "Peer deeply. Tell me what you see."

She complied and to her astonishment found incredible depth. It was like looking into a bottomless canyon. How could she possibly have thought this person shallow, superficial—?

"Jo! Where are you, Jo!"

Joanne spun around in time to see Cliff entering the foyer.

"What are you doing here?"

"I came to see you, what else?"

"You could have at least knocked!" She knew she sounded harsh and furious, but he had come at such a bad time. How was she to explain Erik's presence?

"Why? Are you hiding something—or someone—from me?" Cliff asked suspiciously.

Joanne turned. "Cliff, I want you to meet—" she began, then stopped short. Erik was gone!

"Meet who?" Cliff was frowning.

Where had Erik gone? How could he have disappeared so fast?

"What's going on?" Now Cliff sounded angry.

"Didn't you . . . didn't you see someone when you came in?"

"No. Was I supposed to?" He lifted one eyebrow.

"He . . . he was here a second ago." She looked up at the stairs, wondering how Erik could have run up them without anyone's seeing or hearing him.

"You have a boyfriend stashed away that I don't know about?" Cliff's voice was tight with controlled anger.

"I—I don't know anything anymore. I thought . . . I thought . . ."

"Don't try to deny it. Cindy told me everything."

Joanne stared at him as she gripped the railing of the stairs. She felt as if she were awakening from a dream, a dream that was rapidly eluding her. "What . . . what did Cindy tell you?"

"Don't play dumb with me, Jo! I thought we had something special going."

"We did. I mean, we do."

She looked back at the stairs. "Erik?" she whispered, still unable to grasp what had happened. Had he only existed in her dreams after all?

Where did you go?

"Yeah, Erik. That's the name Cindy told me."

"Cliff, I'm not sure what's happening right

now. But I think maybe you should go now. I want—''

What did she want? Erik to come back? Erik to kiss her?

"I'm not going anywhere until you give me some answers. When did you meet this guy, anyway? Were you seeing him all the while you were going with me? How long have you been seeing him behind my back—?'' He stopped as he realized his voice was rising out of control. He squared his shoulders, lifted his chin, and forced himself to continue in a calmer manner. "You really had me fooled, Jo. I thought you liked me. I know I love you.''

"Love?''

"Yeah. Guess I'm a big idiot.''

"You love me?''

"You heard me the first time. So who is this Erik guy?''

"I told you, I'm not sure. Maybe I dreamt the whole thing. Maybe he's not here at all.''

Cliff eyed her warily. "I think you're putting me on. You were just about to introduce me to him. I think he's hiding somewhere. Well, I'm not gonna go look for him, or fight him, if that's what you're hoping. No way. I'm not going to force you to like me. I just came by to see if what Cindy said was true. Now that I know she wasn't lying, I'll leave you alone with what's-his-name.''

"Cliff, wait a minute—''

It was too late; he was already gone. A moment later, she heard his car start up.

Love. The word echoed in her mind as she listened to the car drive away in the distance.

He loves me.

And I love . . .

"Here, princess."

Erik was back at the top of the stairs. His arms were not extended as before, but his smile was broad, welcoming her.

"Where did you go? How did you disappear so fast?" she asked.

"Let's not worry about trivial details. Let's begin where we left off, before we were so rudely interrupted."

Cliff *loves* me . . .

Erik descended toward her, so smoothly that she wondered if he had actually glided through the air. His feet seemed to have alighted on the step. Or was this just an illusion, her imagination, a trick of light—?

He tilted his head, ready to kiss her.

His lips were not as warm as before. They were cold.

Cliff. I'm sorry. I love you too.

Gently, she pushed Erik away.

"What's wrong, princess?"

She saw disappointment in his eyes—or was it annoyance?

Then she saw his teeth. Funny, they seemed to change each time she looked at them. They reminded her of—what?—vampire's teeth?

Suddenly it occurred to her that what had seemed to alarm him before, had caused him to vanish so abruptly at dawn, was—sunlight!

Was it possible that this stranger before her was actually a . . . ?

"You're tense," he remarked. "Let me help you relax."

"No. Please stay away from me!"

"What's wrong now?"

"Get out of my house!"

"I thought we've already been through this." He moved closer until his body was pressing against hers.

Joanne slid away from him. Remembering her car keys she ran to her room. Shc grabbed her pocketbook and braced herself to push her way back down the stairs. But, to her relief, Erik was already gone.

She bolted out of the house.

Chapter Eleven

No one acknowledged her presence when she entered the police station. A policewoman was at the desk, immersed in a conversation with an elderly man who reeked of beer. Behind the woman was a male officer. He had his back to everyone as he talked in a low voice on the phone.

This is an emergency! Joanne wanted to shout at them. But lacking the courage, she forced herself to be patient and sat in a chair next to a smelly ashtray.

As she waited, she began to lose her nerve. Maybe she had made a mistake coming here. The more she thought about what had happened, the more unbelievable it all seemed. Maybe none of it had happened at all. Maybe it had all only been in her mind.

"May I help you, miss?"

The elderly man had disappeared into another room, and the policewoman was now looking expectantly at her.

"I–I—" Joanne stammered as she approached the desk.

"Is there a problem?" the woman asked impatiently.

"I would like to report a man in my house."

"A man in your house?" the woman echoed, frowning in confusion.

"Yes."

"Could you be more specific? Are you talking about forced entry? Is he still there?"

"No, he didn't force his way in. Yes, he's still there . . . I think."

"You think?"

"He keeps appearing and disappearing, but . . ."

"Look, miss, I haven't all day. I wish you'd make up your mind and tell me exactly what the problem is. Is the man still there or not?"

"I'm not sure. I think he's hiding in my house somewhere. You see, he's no ordinary man. I—or rather, my friend—made the horrible mistake of inviting him into the house. Now I can't seem to get rid of him."

"Why did your friend invite this person into your home?"

"Well, because we were having a party—"

"Party?" the policewoman looked scornful. "Now I know you're wasting our time. Look, miss, this is the Lemore Police Department. We have urgent matters to deal with here—even, in case you're not aware of it, life-and-death situations. I'm sorry, but we simply cannot afford to concern ourselves with boyfriend and girlfriend problems. So if you'd kindly excuse me—"

"You've got it all wrong. It *is* a life-and-death situation. I think the man in my house is—"

The phone rang. The policewoman grabbed the receiver. "Lemore Police Department."

Frustrated, Joanne looked over at the male officer on the other phone. The officer was jotting something down in a notepad on his desk. After he hung up, he gave Joanne a polite, meaningless smile.

Joanne paced the floor. She seriously considered leaving the station. But then why should she? This *was* a life-and-death situation!

"I see you're still here," the policewoman said as she hung up her phone.

Joanne returned to the desk.

"You've got to help me, officer. You've got to get this person out of my house."

"Where are your parents? Are they aware of this . . . er, problem?"

"They are away on vacation."

"I see."

No, you don't! Joanne wanted to scream at her. In a controlled voice, she said, "I have reason to believe that this person in my house is crazy . . . he acts like . . . well . . . a vampire."

The policewoman stared blankly at her, and a corner of her mouth began to twitch. "Did you say a vampire? Why are you certain this person is, ah, a vampire?"

"He seemed to have powers."

"Powers? What kind of powers?"

"He made me fall into some kind of trance."

"Would he by any chance be a great looker?" the woman asked, still straining to keep from laughing.

"Well, he's very handsome," Joanne admitted, "but—"

"I see," the officer interrupted. The smug look on her face was saying: That explains it all. At length, she asked bluntly, "Are you on drugs, young lady?"

"Of course not!"

"Well, in case you haven't heard," she said, "vampires exist only in books and movies."

"I thought that too, until now. This person actually disappeared when he realized it was daylight."

"What did you have at this party?" the policewoman asked.

"Nothing except soft drinks. Besides, that was a couple of nights ago."

The woman looked at her partner, as if to say: What do you think?

He answered her silent question. "I think we should notify her parents. I think we should tell them to keep an eye on this kid." He asked Joanne gruffly, "Why are you out at this time of night? Shouldn't you be studying or getting ready for school tomorrow?"

"Because I'm upset! Because I have a *stranger* in my house!" she shouted, no longer able to control her voice.

"Now, now, take it easy, miss." The woman

reached for a pen. "Just give me the name of your parents and the place they're staying. Then we'll see what we can do."

It was all getting out of hand. Joanne didn't want the police to notify her parents. She just wanted them to get the stranger out of the house.

"What about the prowler that Mrs. Pearl saw?" she asked.

"What are you talking about?"

"Didn't a woman named Mrs. Pearl call you about a prowler the other night?"

The policewoman glanced at a pad on her desk. "Yes. We already checked it out."

"She saw somebody looking in at her from a second story window. Nobody could have looked in without a ladder. Did the police find a ladder?"

"The person could have escaped with the ladder."

"Wouldn't you think someone would have become suspicious and called you if he or she had seen a person running off with a ladder?"

"We ask the questions around here, miss. Now, if you'd kindly cooperate and tell us the name of your parents—"

"Never mind; forget it," Joanne said, backing away from the desk.

"We're only trying to help."

"You don't believe a word I said. You want to call my parents and tell them to put me in a hospital or clinic. You think I'm either crazy or on drugs."

Before either of them could stop her, she turned on her heels and fled the station. When she was back inside her car, she knew she had made a fool of herself with the police. Why hadn't she behaved more calmly? Running away from them like that had only convinced them that she was indeed looney.

She drove aimlessly all night, trying to decide what to do next. How could she get rid of that guy, of a vampire? she asked herself over and over. The following morning she parked her car at the side of the road, at a quiet spot near a park, and slept for a while. When she woke up, she was hungry. She drove to a Burger King restaurant, where most of the kids from school usually hung out.

The restaurant was fairly empty, since it was during school. Joanne sat in her favorite booth and ate only half of a salad. After a few bites she realized she wasn't as hungry as she thought. She was still upset from her ordeal with the police and the stranger in her house. She desperately needed someone to talk with, especially someone who would not smirk or frown at her.

Maybe she should call her parents, after all. It wasn't every day that one had a monster in her house. This certainly would be a good excuse to interrupt a vacation.

"Hey, wake up! You're a million miles away!" Cindy said.

Joanne looked up in surprise. She had been so deep in thought she hadn't seen her best friend come into the restaurant. Now the place was rapidly filling up. Had school let out already? Without realizing it, she had been sitting here for hours!

"How time flies when you're having fun," she muttered dryly.

Cindy slid into the seat across from her. "How come you weren't in school today? And, not to be hateful, but you look terrible, Jo!"

"That's because I feel terrible! Oh, Cindy, I don't know what to do."

"Well, for starters you can tell me what the hell is going on between you and Cliff. And who is this Erik guy you've been talking about on the phone?"

"Erik is the one who's been hiding in my house."

"You mean he's the one we heard that night?"

"I think so."

"You're in *love* with him?" Cindy asked incredulously.

"No, I'm not in love with him. I only thought I was at the time. He made me think I was. He hypnotized me or something. And then Cliff came over, and— Oh, it's all so horrible! Now I think Cliff hates me. I'm going to have to talk to him, make him understand what really happened."

"Hey, slow down. You're confusing me. So you're saying you're *not* in love with this Erik?"

"Right. It's Cliff I love. I don't know why I even doubted it for a second."

Cindy pulled a face. "Jeez, I messed things up, didn't I? I should've never told Cliff. The reason I did was because I hated seeing the two of you apart. I could tell you weren't in your right mind when I called you, and I honestly thought you were drinking or something. So I told Cliff to check it out. I'm sorry."

"Sorry? You did me a favor. If Cliff hadn't come when he did—God, I don't know what would've happened. Seeing him was like a slap in the face, Cindy. He woke me up."

"Who is this Erik?" Cindy whispered, after a thoughtful pause. "Where did he come from?"

"I'm not sure." Joanne was reluctant to express her theory about Erik—not after the way the police officers had treated her.

"I don't want to scare you, Jo, but I think I should tell you what my mother just heard on the radio."

Joanne looked at her. She could tell by her friend's tone that she was about to hear something horrible.

"A man has escaped from the mental institution," Cindy went on. "They say he's very dangerous. He killed his mother and sister seven years ago when he was a teenager. It was one of the most violent murder cases in the history of the state. They say only a really crazy person could've done what he did."

"What do you mean?" Joanne could scarcely hear her own voice.

"They say he killed his mother and sister and drank their blood. Then he put them in garbage bags and buried them in the woods in back of his house."

"How gross!"

"No kidding. And now he's loose."

"But the institution is far from here, at least two hundred and fifty miles."

"I know, but he could have easily hitched a ride. He could be anywhere. He could be . . . here at Lemore."

"What does this guy look like? Did anyone say?"

"Not really, except that he was young, somewhere in his early twenties."

Erik's age.

"Do you suppose . . . do you think . . ." Cindy couldn't finish, but Joanne knew what she was trying to say.

"I don't know, Cindy. I'm positive about one thing, though. Erik isn't normal. Whether he's a crazed killer or a—well, never mind. The important thing is, I've got to get him out of my house."

"What were you going to say?"

"Nothing."

"Why won't you tell me? I thought I was your best friend."

"You are, silly. It's just that . . . I had an awful experience with the police. I don't think I could take it if you laughed at me too."

"The police!" Cindy exclaimed in surprise. "And they didn't help you?"

Now Joanne knew she had let too much slip out. Cindy would never leave her alone until she told her everything.

"They thought I was on drugs or something when I told them I thought Erik was— Oh, Cindy, you must promise not to laugh!"

Cindy nodded eagerly. "You know me better than that."

"Well, remember the noise we heard the other night at my house? I finally found out what it was. It was a black bird. It wasn't an ordinary bird, though." She swallowed, then braced herself. "Cindy, I told the police I think Erik's a vampire, and he's living in my house."

Cindy looked at her—the same blank look the policewoman had given her earlier. Just as the policewoman's had done, Cindy's mouth began to twitch.

"I knew you would laugh!" Joanne said, flaring. She jumped to her feet.

"Wait!" Cindy seized her hand before she could run off. "Sit back down. I'm not laughing. Really, Jo, I'm not."

Joanne could feel all eyes in the restaurant turn toward her. Embarrassed, she slipped back into her seat.

"I know it's hard to believe," she admitted. "I can't believe it myself. But it seems to fit. I felt like I'd fallen so ridiculously in love with him it was as though he'd cast a spell. And you should have seen the look on his face when he saw sunlight in the window. I know it's not much to go on, but who else except a vampire is afraid of sunlight?"

"I don't know. But *vampires*?" Cindy shook her head incredulously, then studied Joanne with sudden concern. "Gee, Jo, I've never seen you so scared. You should see yourself. You're so white.

You definitely look as if you've had the fright of your life."

"Yeah, well, I guess I should be grateful you're not laughing," Joanne muttered as she stared gloomily at her soft drink. Maybe I should commit myself to that mental hospital two hundred and fifty miles away, she thought. Maybe I am actually losing my mind.

"Jo?" Cindy said after a long silence.

"What?"

"I can't leave you looking so scared like this. Whatever is it that's in your house, I'm going to help you get rid of it."

Chapter Twelve

"A vampire?" Cliff laughed.

Joanne and Cindy had come to see Cliff at his house, hoping he'd somehow help them with the stranger in Joanne's home.

"You've got to believe me," Joanne pleaded. "I think he had me in some kind of trance. He made me think I was in love with him. He hypnotized me or something. Vampires do that, you know. They put people under their spells and then—and then—" Her voice broke as tears rushed to her eyes.

"Hey, don't . . . don't start crying on me," Cliff pleaded.

"Can't you see she's telling the truth?" Cindy said.

"Cliff, I don't want us to break up." Joanne choked back her tears and spoke in a stronger voice. "It's the last thing in the world I want. I . . . love you, Cliff."

Cliff pulled her into his arms, and for a long moment they didn't say anything, holding each other.

"But a vampire," he whispered incredulously when they finally broke free. "That's a hard one to swallow."

"Can't you see how scared Jo is?" Cindy pointed out. "Obviously she has been through something terrible. Look at how awful she looks!"

"Cindy, I wish you'd stop saying that," Joanne told her.

"Cindy's right," Cliff regarded Joanne solicitously. "Tell me everything that happened."

"It was horrible, Cliff." She took in a deep breath, then told him about her encounter with Erik, about how he had filled the room with the foul-smelling mist, and about how the bird had guarded the phone. "He disappeared into thin air when he saw daylight coming through the window," she finished.

Cliff let out a low whistle. "Incredible."

"Well, do you believe her?" Cindy demanded.

He was silent for a long moment. "Where do you think he is now?" he asked.

"Inside my house somewhere," Joanne said.

"Where inside, do you think?"

"I don't know."

"If he's a vampire, he'd be in a dark, secret place."

"Well, do you believe her or not?" Cindy asked again.

"Seeing is believing," he finally answered. "Come on, let's check this out while it's still daylight."

Ten minutes later they were at Joanne's house.

"Where do you want to look first?" Cliff asked.

"Both the cellar and the attic are dark," Joanne said. "So I guess he could be in either place."

"We'll try the cellar first. Vampires are usually in basements, I think."

As the trio began to descend the steep wooden stairs, Cindy whispered, "This reminds me of a movie I saw about vampires once. They were in the cellar of an old house, and in order to protect themselves while they slept during daylight hours, they set booby traps near their coffins."

Joanne and Cliff stopped short.

"Booby traps?" Joanne echoed.

"Yes," Cindy said. "At the bottom of the stairs there was a bear trap. The man in the movie stepped right into it and almost lost his foot. Near the coffin there was a button on the floor. If you stepped on this button, a gun on a wall would go off. The gun was precisely aimed to blow off a person's head."

The overhead light was on, but it scarcely lit the huge cellar. Cliff carefully swept the floor with the light from one of the three flashlights he had taken from his house, and Joanne used her flashlight to examine the fieldstone walls. Cindy scanned the beamed ceiling with hers.

The furnace at the far end of the cellar kicked on, startling them all.

"Dad's always complaining about that furnace,'' Joanne said in a shaky voice. ''Sometimes it wakes us all up in the middle of the night. Someday he's going to get it fixed. Either that or buy a new one.'' Although she knew she was rambling, she couldn't stop herself. ''There's a lot of junk down here, isn't there?''

Cliff said nothing as his flashlight beam ran along a cluttered workbench, lawn mower, rakes, shovel, and a pile of old automobile tires.

''One of these days we're going to have to clean out this mess,'' Joanne said, as she carefully picked her way through the cellar. ''We could have quite a garage sale, make some money . . .''

''Everything's down here except a coffin,'' Cindy cut in.

Cliff paused in the middle of the room. ''Yeah,'' he agreed. ''I don't think anyone's sleeping down here.''

Joanne caught the skepticism in his voice. ''We didn't check the other end of the cellar,'' she reminded him. ''Besides, who said he's in a coffin?''

''Vampires always sleep in coffins,'' Cindy said. ''Don't they?''

Joanne ignored the question. ''Wouldn't it be terribly awkward to carry a coffin in here?'' she pointed out. ''Wouldn't somebody have noticed?''

''Not if he'd brought it in here in the middle of night,'' Cliff said.

''Maybe any enclosure would do,'' Joanne went on. ''As long as it's dark and he's protected and hidden.''

''You mean like a closet?'' Cindy whispered.

"Yes."

"In other words, he could be anywhere in this house," Cliff said.

"Yes."

The three continued the exploration of the cellar in silence. When they reached the other end, they noticed it wasn't as gloomy here. Dusty light, piercing through a small casement window, feebly illuminated the area.

"There's too much light here," Cliff said. "We need to look where it's completely dark."

"There're no windows in the attic," Joanne told him.

"Okay, let's go up and check it out."

A few minutes later they were under the trap door that led to the attic. Joanne pulled down the ladder, then braced herself as she followed Cliff up it.

"Where's the switch to the light?" he asked as he disappeared into the darkness above.

"It's on the wall to your right," Joanne told him. Cindy clung closely behind her.

Cliff searched for the switch with his flashlight, found it, and flipped it. Nothing happened.

"The bulb must've burned out," he said as he swept the low, slanted ceiling with the flashlight beam. He located a dangling light fixture, but the socket was empty.

"Somebody forgot to put a bulb in," he said.

"No, somebody broke the bulb," Cindy said as she shined her flashlight down on a glittering collection of shards by her feet.

Joanne knew who had broken the light bulb. "Erik," she whispered.

"What?" Cliff said.

"I think Erik deliberately broke it . . . to keep his place dark and safe."

"In other words, you're pretty sure he's up here."

Joanne's glance took in the blackness around her; it was so thick, so deep. "Yes."

Her certainty caused Cliff and Cindy to feel uncertain. They moved closer to Joanne and listened intently.

"It's awfully quiet up here," Cindy said.

"How big is this attic?" Cliff's flashlight could only reach so far.

"It's the whole length of the house," Joanne said. "It's as big as the cellar."

"Maybe we should go back down and get another light bulb," Cindy suggested.

"No need," Cliff said. "We'll just stick together and use our flashlights."

"Watch out for booby traps," Cindy reminded them.

Gingerly, the three threaded their way through the attic. There was more clutter up here than in the cellar and there seemed to be more cobwebs, perhaps because of the low, peaked ceiling. More than once Joanne found herself peeling sticky strands away from her face and hair.

"What's this?" Cliff asked, pointing his flashlight at a door.

"It's a closet."

"What's in it?"

"Old clothes, I think." It had been a long time since Joanne was up here in the attic. As far as she knew, this closet could be empty right now. Her mother was always giving old things away to various charities.

"Is it deep?" Cliff asked.

"Deep enough," Joanne assured him, knowing he was wondering if it was large enough to accommodate a sleeping person.

Cliff hesitated a beat, then reached for the door handle.

"I'm scared!" Cindy suddenly cried out from behind them, recoiling from the closet.

Joanne remained at Cliff's side. Swallowing, she nodded at him to proceed.

Slowly, Cliff opened the door.

More darkness greeted them. Joanne felt some of the tension leave her; she'd been so certain something would leap out at them from the closet.

"You're right—old clothes," Cliff said, shining the flashlight into its inky depths.

He stepped back and was closing the door when Joanne spotted a dark bulk at the far end.

"What's this?"

"What? Where?" Cliff swiftly swept the darkness with light.

Joanne pointed, and Cliff's flashlight followed her finger.

"Looks like some kind of wooden trunk," he said, moving closer toward the black bulk.

"I don't remember ever seeing it before."

"Maybe it—it's the coffin." Cindy's voice was shaky.

"It's too small."

"Maybe he sleeps in a fetal position," Cindy suggested.

Joanne shuddered at the thought. She could picture it perfectly: Erik, at sunlight, returning to death or birth—depending how one looked at it—inside a dark enclosure, inside a womb. Somehow it seemed more likely than his sleeping in a supine position.

"You sure you've never seen it before?" she heard Cliff whisper.

She shook her head, unable to speak.

"You think we've finally found him?" Cindy asked.

She didn't answer, didn't have to. They stared at the trunk until the flashlight in Joanne's hand shook too much for them to see clearly.

Cliff crept toward the trunk, pushing aside the clothes on the rack.

"Be careful," Joanne cautioned.

He paused before the trunk, waited as he gathered more courage, then positioned his flashlight directly above the lid.

"Here goes!" He reached for the lid.

Joanne held her breath, then squeezed her eyes shut. Maybe she should yell at Cliff not to open it. Maybe it wasn't such a good idea. Maybe they would be opening a Pandora's box or something. Maybe they would be releasing unspeakable evil into the world and—

"You can open your eyes now," Cliff said, quietly breaking her thoughts.

"What? Did you already—?" She looked at the trunk; it was still closed. She looked at Cliff, puzzled.

"It's locked from the inside."

Chapter Thirteen

"What do we do now?" Joanne asked.

"Maybe I could force it open," Cliff suggested. "Do you have a crowbar in the house?"

"Maybe that wouldn't be such a good idea. Maybe we should just get out of here, talk this over first."

Cliff quickly complied, Cindy nodding in agreement behind him. Within minutes the group was inside Cliff's car.

"I don't believe it." Cindy looked as if she were going to be sick. Her face was as white as milk—and so were Cliff's and Joanne's.

"We haven't really found anything," Cliff assured them, although his tone wasn't convincing. "An old trunk doesn't prove anything. Maybe Jo just hasn't noticed it was there all along."

"I was up there last week," Joanne suddenly remembered. "I was in that closet with my mother, helping her pack for the vacation. That trunk wasn't there then. I would've noticed it—it's certainly big enough. And besides, I used to play in that closet when I was little. I used to try on old clothes and play grown-up. I've never seen that trunk."

"Then it must be Erik's," Cindy concluded.

Joanne and Cliff looked at her. The silence in the car was suddenly deafening.

Unable to endure the silence any longer, Joanne said, "We've got to get it out of the house."

"Maybe we should give the trunk to the police," Cindy suggested. "Have them open it."

"That's a crazy idea," Cliff said.

"I don't know about that," Joanne disagreed. "They laughed at me, thought I was drinking or on drugs. Proof like this would teach them a few things."

"I don't know." Cliff shook his head doubtfully. "We won't know anything until we open that chest."

"But I don't want you to open it," Joanne told him. "What if he is in there and he jumps up and grabs you. That's what vampires do, isn't it—kill people who disturb them?"

"Oh, all right," Cliff relented, "we'll have the police handle it."

At the police station the policewoman immediately recognized Joanne. When she heard the story of the mysterious trunk and the suspicion that a body was inside it, she laughed openly. But after her laughter subsided, she promised to dispatch someone to Joanne's house for a quick look. Now Joanne knew it was an empty promise. An hour had passed, and the police still hadn't arrived at her house.

She called from Cliff's house, and the policewoman said, "An emergency came up. Don't worry, honey, we'll get to it . . . eventually."

Furious, Joanne slammed the phone down.

"What's the matter, Jo?" Cliff asked.

"The police don't believe us. They're just putting us off."

"Maybe you should call your parents, Jo," Cindy suggested.

"I hate to do that. I really wanted to prove that I could handle this by myself."

"I think this is really out of our league," Cindy told her.

"Don't you think it's also out of my parents' league? I'm sure they don't know anything more about vampires than we do."

"So what we need," Cliff said thoughtfully, "is to find someone who's an expert on vampires. We need a vampire killer."

"Do you want me to get you the phone directory?" Joanne offered sardonically.

Ignoring the remark, Cliff pulled at his lower lip. After a lengthy pause, he said, "If we can't find an expert, then we'll just have to become experts ourselves."

"What are you talking about?" Joanne demanded.

"Come on, let's go to the library. We're going to learn everything we can about vampires."

Five minutes later they were in the tomblike silence of the Lemore Public Library. The librarian, a short, frail woman with thick spectacles, looked at them oddly when they asked for books on vampires, but she quickly led them to the occult/mysticism section at the back of the library. There it seemed more private and dimmer, since the light from the central ceiling fixture did not quite reach the corners.

Joanne, Cliff, and Cindy scanned the shelves, collecting all the books they could find on vampirism. They were surprised to see so many titles on the subject: *The Vampire in Legend, Fact and Art; Lust for Blood: The Consuming Story of Vampires; The Natural History of the Vampires; Night Creatures; The Dracula Myth; Were-Wolf and Vampire in Romania; The Vampire: His Kith and Kin . . .*

When they felt they had selected enough, they sat around a small wooden table to peruse their findings.

"Look at this," Cliff said, sliding a book toward Joanne and Cindy. Together, they read:

"Vampires were skilled at changing shapes. They did not, as is sometimes believed, change into bats. This metamorphosis was a literary invention, added to vampire tales after the discovery of New World bats that fed on blood. But to move undetected from place to place, vampires could dissolve to dust or mist, sail through the air as owls and run along the ground as wolves or cats . . ."

Joanne felt a chill as her eyes gazed on a picture

of a cat with golden eyes, fangs, and deep black fur.

"What's the matter, Jo?" Cliff asked. "You look as if you're about to faint."

"I–I saw a cat like this. It was on the couch. I chased it off and it disappeared up the stairs."

"Listen to this," Cindy said, then read aloud from a book in front of her: *"A vampire can control the weather over short distances. He can raise up storms, winds, blizzards, and the like. He can bend the laws of nature."*

"Is there anything he can't do?" Joanne said.

No one answered her. Cliff opened another book and found an interesting yet disturbing passage. *"A vampire is not a demon,"* he read. *"Nor is he a ghost or a devil, although he works with other evil forces. He is nothing but a corpse. He is a dead body that maintains a semblance of life by drinking living blood."*

Joanne turned a page in the book she was reading. A picture of a beautiful woman with glazed eyes and blood dripping from one corner of her red lips stared back at her. The woman's skin looked cold and white as milk. Was she alive? Half-alive?

"Do you become a vampire when a vampire bites you?" Joanne asked.

"I'm not sure. I think so," Cindy said.

Cliff showed them another page. "Well, according to this, the victim becomes a vampire only if he dies. A lot of blood has to be taken from him first. In other words, he has to bleed to death. When he finally dies, he comes back from the dead—as a vampire.''

''I don't think I want to read any more of this,'' Joanne said.

''Me neither,'' Cindy agreed, closing her book.

An uneasy silence fell among them as they returned the books to the shelves.

''The books said vampires can transform themselves into animals—which was exactly what the man in your house did,'' Cindy said.

Outside the library, the three were astonished to find the day almost gone. Shadows were long, and the sun was beginning to sink behind the trees.

''I'm going to be late for supper,'' Cindy declared. ''My mother will kill me. She's worried enough as it is because of that guy who escaped from the mental institution.''

''And I'm supposed to be at work in half an hour,'' Cliff said, glancing at his watch. He was a part-time attendant at a gasoline service station.

He and Cindy hurried toward his car, then stopped short as a thought simultaneously occurred to them.

''Jo, you can't go home now,'' Cindy said.

''It'll be dark soon and . . .'' Cliff's voice trailed away.

''He'll be up and waiting for me,'' Joanne finished flatly.

''Maybe I should take the night off,'' Cliff said. ''It won't hurt the gas station any. Who knows, maybe it'll be slow tonight and my partner will be able to handle it alone.''

''No, Cliff. You can't afford to lose that job.''

Joanne knew he was trying hard to save enough money for college. His father had been laid off from his job last year, and Cliff didn't want to be an extra financial burden to his parents.

"I can always find another job," Cliff said.

"It's not that easy, and you know it."

"You can stay at my house," Cindy offered.

"Are you sure your mother won't mind?" Joanne asked. "I won't eat supper. I just want a place to stay until morning."

"Don't be silly!"

On the porch at Cindy's house Cliff held Joanne in his arms, as though afraid to leave her. The sun was now completely gone, and the numerous shadows on the ground had blended into a single, endless mass.

"I'm so glad we're back together." His voice was husky yet soft in her hair. "Promise me you won't leave here until I come back from work?"

"I've no intention of going back home in the dark, if that's what you're afraid of."

"Good. When I come back we'll decide what to do. We'll get rid of that . . . that creature in your house."

Joanne's eyes were closed as she rested her head against his shoulder. When she reopened them, she was surprised to find a change in the air. It seemed thicker, seemed to be rolling and gathering like a mist.

Vampires could dissolve to dust or mist.

"A fog seems to be developing," she said.

Cliff followed her gaze. The mist appeared to

be growing, at the same time deepening in color, turning from white to gray.

"Do you think it's him?" she whispered.

"I don't know. Maybe not. Maybe it's just an ordinary fog. Have you heard the weather report?"

"No."

Together, they watched the mist for a moment. When nothing further happened, Cliff gave Joanne a tender kiss, then headed for his car in the driveway.

"Cliff!" Joanne shouted after him.

"What?"

"Call me as soon as you get to work."

"Sure."

As he drove away, she eyed the mist once again. It still hadn't changed. Only an ordinary mist, she told herself.

She hurried inside the house.

Chapter Fourteen

When Joanne pulled back the curtain to look out the window, the mist was gone.

"What are you looking at?" Cindy asked behind her.

"There was a heavy mist out there a minute ago. I was wondering if it was you-know-who."

"Do you think he's *following* us?" Alarm showed in her huge brown eyes.

"I don't know. Maybe I'm just being paranoid now. It could've been just an ordinary fog."

"It doesn't look like we're having the kind of weather for a fog."

"Let's forget about it," Joanne said. "It was a fog, and now it's gone. Let's get our minds on something else. Do you have any ideas? Is anything good on TV tonight? How about a game of Scrabble?"

"Jo!" Cindy's younger sister, Hannah, squealed with delight as she came into the room. "Look what I got for my birthday!" In her arms was a cloth doll with triangular eyes, painted smile, and long hair made out of cherry-red yarn.

"Oh, she's so cute!" Joanne said, smiling.

Hannah beamed proudly, then hurried out of the room, hugging the doll. As she left, her mother emerged.

"Why, hello, Joanne."

"Hi, Mrs. Harris." Joanne felt awkward as she remembered she'd behaved like a spoiled child the last time she'd seen Mrs. Harris.

"I'm so sorry I didn't make you feel welcome the other evening," Mrs. Harris apologized, sensing Joanne's unease. "It's just that I had so much to do, with Hannah's birthday party and all. I believe she actually invited the entire elementary school."

The incident seemed so long ago now; so much had happened since then.

"I understand, Mrs. Harris."

"I invited her to stay over tonight, Mom," Cindy said. "Is that okay?"

"Of course, dear." Mrs. Harris gave Joanne a warm, affectionate smile, then disappeared into another room.

Joanne began to feel guilty. Was she subjecting Cindy and her family to horrible dangers? She would never forgive herself if something happened to any of them.

"Come on, I bought a new tape," Cindy said,

already heading for her room. "You're going to like it. It's great!"

Joanne nervously glanced out the window one more time, then followed her friend.

The hours crawled by. Joanne tried to lose herself to conversation, music, and a game of Scrabble, but she could not stop looking out the window or listening for telltale sounds. She was confident Erik was nearby, somewhere just out of sight, somewhere watching her.

"We know too much," she blurted out in the middle of Scrabble.

"What are you talking about?"

"To keep us from talking, he might want to get rid of us."

"I wish you hadn't said that!"

"I'm sorry. Maybe I should go home, or at least go someplace where I wouldn't be putting you and the others in danger."

"Don't try to be a big hero. It's too dangerous, Jo. We have to stick together, form something like an army."

"I suppose you're right, but what if something happens to—"

The phone rang, startling her into silence.

"It's for you, Jo," Cindy said after she answered it. "It's Cliff."

"Are you all right?" Jo asked him as soon as she grabbed the receiver.

"Sure," Cliff answered. "What did you think would happen to me?"

"Remember that mist we saw on the porch earlier? It disappeared as soon as you left. I was afraid that maybe . . ."

"It followed me?" Cliff finished for her.

"Yes."

"It did."

Joanne stared stupidly at the phone.

"Jo, are you still there?"

"I'm here. What . . . what do you mean it followed you, Cliff?"

"The fog, or whatever the hell it was, stayed around the car. I had to use my windshield wipers to see. And because I couldn't see where I was going, I had to drive slowly. You wouldn't believe how cold that thing was, Jo! I could see my own breath, which kept clouding the windshield, making it even more difficult to see."

"Then what happened?"

"Well, I decided I'd better get moving before this thing began to seep into the car. So I took a chance and stepped on the gas. Just as I hoped, I drove out of it. When I looked back in the rearview mirror, there was nothing behind me. It was as if I had imagined the whole thing. It was really weird, Jo—spooky."

"Where are you now?"

"At the station. I'm starting to close up now."

"I told you to call me right away."

"I know, but you wouldn't believe how busy it got around here. I just didn't have a chance until now. How's everything with you and Cindy? Do you want me to come over after I finish up?"

"Nothing's out of the ordinary here," she assured him. "I suppose there's no reason for you to come here. Cindy's mother is being exceptionally nice to me. She might get suspicious and ask a lot of questions if you come over now."

After she hung up, she found herself feeling worse instead of better. Although she was relieved that Cliff was safe, she was upset about the mist. It had *followed* him! This meant her fear wasn't groundless.

She had put her friends in danger.

Cindy was surprised to find her friend fast asleep. The two of them had been reading magazines, she on the rug on the floor and Joanne on the bed. Now Cindy looked over at the clock. It was almost midnight. So far, the night had been uneventful—to her relief.

Quietly, she covered Joanne with a blanket. Joanne was sleeping peacefully now, but when she was awake her eyes had been wild with fear, and she hadn't been able to stop trembling. Cindy felt a pang of guilt. This whole thing was all her fault. She should never have insisted on that stupid party!

She looked in the mirror over her dresser. Pimples were starting to break out along her forehead. Earlier this would have been a major crisis, but now it all seemed so unimportant. She sighed, and then she heard a soft tapping sound.

She pivoted. Everything seemed unchanged. Yet she was certain the noise had been in this room.

She looked over at the window. Had she heard someone knocking on the glass?

No. It was only her imagination—which was to be expected. They'd all had a frightful day today.

Quickly, she turned off the light and joined her friend in the big bed. She stared at the window. A half-moon illuminated a thick tree branch outside the house. Maybe this was what she'd heard against the glass. Maybe it was windy outside and the wind was slapping the branch against the window.

She closed her eyes and fell asleep.

Then she heard the soft sounds again. *Tap . . . tap tap . . . tap . . .*

Was this happening in her dream, or was she really hearing it? She couldn't remember opening her eyes, although she was now looking at the window again. She could see the big branch, and something else.

She narrowed her eyes, straining to see more clearly. The puzzling object was oval, its features hidden in the moonlight.

Something else appeared next to the oval object, something spidery. As it touched the glass, Cindy realized it was a hand with lengthy fingers.

Tap . . . tap tap . . .

And the oval thing beside it was a face.

The instant she realized this, she was able to discern its features. It was a young man's face, and his eyes were fixed on her, his mouth moving, forming words that she strangely yearned to hear, but couldn't.

Getting out of bed, she moved closer to the window. Now she could see the face much better. Dimly, she knew she should be frightened, yet she wasn't. She told herself it was because she was dreaming. Nothing, in a physical sense, happened in dreams.

She tried to read the man's lips.

Let me in, he seemed to be saying. *Please, let me in.*

Then he smiled at her, and she smiled back. He was so handsome.

"I'm cold out here," he whispered.

The clarity of his words surprised her. Had she actually heard his voice with her ears, or had her mind heard it?

"Who are you? What are you doing here?" she demanded, her own voice a whisper.

"You know who I am."

"I can't let you in."

"Why not?"

"Because . . . because . . ." Her mind was foggy; only the young man's enchanting face filled it.

"Do not be afraid. I want to help you."

"Help me?"

"I know how it feels to be an outsider. I know how it feels not to be popular."

"You do?"

"Of course." He smiled warmly. "If you let me in, we will talk about it. I will show you how to . . . belong."

"You will?"

"Yes, lovely one. All you have to do is trust me and let me in."

Nothing physical happens in dreams, she reminded herself. She could open the window and it wouldn't matter, because she wouldn't really be opening it.

"Yes," the man urged eagerly, sensing her thoughts. "Open it and I will show you how it feels to belong. Yes."

She moved closer to the window, unlocked it, and started to push it upward.

"No!" Joanne suddenly shouted from behind her.

Startled, Cindy spun around. What was her friend doing here? Then, in a rush, it came to her.

Filled with sudden, stark horror, Cindy jumped away from the window. She couldn't believe it! She had almost let a stranger into her own room!

She ran to her friend's side. When she looked back, the face in the window was gone.

Chapter Fifteen

Neither Joanne nor Cindy had slept after seeing the face in the window. When morning came, it was with steady, dreary rain.

"I have a big test today in math," Cindy suddenly remembered. "If I flunk it, I'll have to take the whole subject over again this summer."

Joanne didn't want to miss any more school either. "I guess we could wait until after school to go back to the house," she said.

But after their last class of the day they met Cliff.

"Today's the day I take my mother grocery shopping," he said. "Since Mom doesn't drive, I take her every week," he added, nodding towards Cindy.

"That's okay," Joanne told him. "We'll wait until you come back."

That was at three o'clock. Now it was after four.

"What's taking him so long?" Cindy asked.

"I suppose there's no hurry," Joanne said. "We could always go back to my house tomorrow."

"Are you kidding? What makes you think this Erik won't come after us again tonight? Oh, we should've skipped school! After all, what's more important, our grades or our lives?"

"Calm down, Cindy. Everything's going to be all right. You'll see."

At Cindy's living room window they watched for Cliff to arrive. The gloomy, relentless rain ran down the glass in blurry streams, at times making it impossible to see out. Finally, Cliff's car pulled into the driveway.

"Sorry for being so late," he said after they ran from the house and were climbing into the car. "Mom bumped into some old friends of hers. I couldn't pull her away from them."

"I think we still have enough time," Joanne said.

"Exactly what are we going to do?" Cliff said as he backed out of the driveway and headed for Joanne's house.

"I'm not sure. I only know that we must get that coffin out of the house. Do you have any ideas?"

"You don't know for sure it's a coffin," Cliff reminded her.

"Trunk, coffin, whatever. It has to go!"

"Well, if we can't bring the police to the vampire,'' Cindy said from the back seat, ''then we'll have to bring the vampire to the police.''

''And how do we do that?''

''Simple. We'll put the coffin, I mean trunk, in the car and take it to the station.''

Joanne stared at her, unable to believe her ears.

''Do you guys have a better idea?''

''What if the police open up the trunk and find nothing but a bunch of old clothes?'' Cliff asked. ''We'll be the laughingstock of Lemore!''

''At this point I don't care if the police laugh at us,'' Joanne said. ''That's all they seem to know how to do anyway.''

''Maybe we should force it open first,'' Cliff suggested. ''And if we don't like what we see, then we'll take it to the police.''

''No.'' Joanne was adamant. ''Too dangerous. Let's just take the trunk to the station.''

''O-kaay,'' Cliff conceded, although his tone made it clear he didn't like the idea. ''It's your trunk.''

Below the attic trapdoor in Joanne's house, Cliff gave each girl a flashlight. ''Ready?'' he said.

Joanne gripped the flashlight tightly. ''Yes.''

''I'm not,'' Cindy said. ''I'm scared.''

''We outnumber him three to one,'' Cliff reminded her. ''We'll be all right.''

''But he has powers,'' Cindy said. ''He can turn into things.''

''Not during the day, Cindy. A vampire—if it is a vampire—is a creature of darkness. Everything's on our side right now.''

He pulled down the stairs to the attic. As

before, the room was in total darkness. The three flashlights scarcely penetrated it.

Rigid with fear, Joanne followed Cliff, while Cindy followed her.

"It seems darker today," Cindy said.

"It's only our imagination," Joanne assured her.

When they reached the closet, they paused. Each seemed to be thinking: there's still time to change our minds.

Cliff opened the door, pushed back the clothes on the rack, and aimed his flashlight at the back of the closet. The trunk was where they'd last seen it.

The trio stared at the wooden chest for a long time, as though it were a bomb that needed to be removed from the premises. Then Cliff reached for the side handle and dragged it out of the closet, careful not to bump anything.

"Jeez, you wouldn't believe how heavy it is!" he exclaimed in a low whisper. "Guess it isn't a bunch of old clothes after all."

"Do you think he can hear us?" Joanne asked, matching his voice.

"Hope not," he replied. "I heard vampires are sound sleepers. Come on, you two, help me with this. Lift up the other end."

With Cindy, Joanne grabbed the opposite side handle on the trunk. She, too, was surprised to find it so heavy.

"Ready?" Cliff asked. When the girls nodded, he led the way toward the stairs. The side handle bit into Joanne's fingers, hurting her, but she forced herself to hold on.

As they descended the stairs, the pain became unbearable. She glanced over at Cindy and Cliff. Both were grimacing with pain.

"Maybe we should stop for a minute," Cindy suggested.

As she said this, Cliff's fingers slipped and his side of the trunk crashed to the floor.

Joanne's instinct was to drop her side and run. Certainly the vampire within would wake up and get them. Yet she and Cindy held on, while Cliff stared at the trunk, waiting to see if it would pop open. When nothing happened, he lifted his end of the trunk again and resumed his descent of the stairs.

"Careful, careful," he muttered to himself as well as to the girls behind him.

When they reached the hallway, they set the trunk down. They waited for their strength to return, then continued onward. Halfway down the second flight of stairs, they felt movement within the trunk.

"He's waking up!" Cindy cried.

"Shhh!" Cliff demanded silence.

The trio paused, on the alert to flee if something should burst from the trunk. Joanne's heart pounded furiously.

The trunk remained still.

"Well, Cliff, *now* do you believe something alive is in there?" she asked.

Still gawking at the trunk, he gave her a faint nod.

"Maybe we should forget this whole thing," Cindy whispered.

"We're more than half done," Cliff said, at last pulling his gaze away from the wooden box. "Once we get it into the car, we'll be okay."

They managed the second flight of stairs, then carried the trunk across the small foyer and out the front door. Joanne was relieved to be outside. At least now the monster was out of her house!

When they reached the car, they carefully lowered the wooden chest into the car's trunk. And when the car's trunk was closed and locked, the three teenagers simultaneously sighed with relief.

Then Joanne looked nervously at the sky.

"We'd better hurry," she said. "It's already starting to get dark."

Chapter Sixteen

"I think I heard something," Cindy said from the back seat of Cliff's car.

Joanne, sitting in the front with Cliff, turned around. "What did you hear?"

"It was a thump . . . from the trunk."

"Maybe it's nothing," Cliff told her, sounding more hopeful than confident. "It's still daylight. The vampire won't wake up."

"How can you tell?" Joanne asked. "It's raining and it's after five o'clock—"

"Did you hear that?" Cindy interrupted. "It's that thumping noise again. Oh Joanne, he *is* waking up! What are we going to do?"

"We're almost there," Cliff said.

It wasn't true. The police station was at least another five miles away.

Joanne glanced at the speedometer. The needle was rising rapidly.

"Slow down, Cliff. The last thing we need now is a car accident."

"Rats!" he suddenly cursed under his breath. Up ahead the traffic beacon had turned red.

"We all need to calm down," Joanne said when the car halted at the light. "Otherwise we're going to do something stupid, something we'll regret."

"Jo's right," Cliff conceded. "Let's not panic. We'll be at the station in a few more minutes."

"That's easy for you guys to say," Cindy said. "I'm the one sitting closest to that thing in there."

The light changed to green and the car shot forward. "Almost there," Cliff muttered, his face grim and tight with determination.

"I smell something," Cindy suddenly declared. "It smells as if something's gone bad."

"I don't smell anything," Joanne said.

"It seems to be everywhere . . . all around me." Cindy cupped her nose with her hand. "It's *horrible*, Jo!"

Now Joanne and Cliff caught a whiff of the smell.

"Roll down the windows!" Cliff ordered.

The stench faded somewhat after the windows were down, but it remained strong near Cindy. "It seems to be coming from under the seat," she said.

"A few more miles," Cliff repeated. "A few more miles and we'll be home free."

"Something's happening," Cindy said, looking down at the seat.

Yellowish vapor was seeping through the cushions beneath her. It was faint, barely detectable. Joanne had to look twice before she could see it.

"He's coming in!" Cindy cried. "Cliff, stop the car! He's coming in!"

The instant Cliff pulled over, Cindy jumped out of the car.

"What's going on?" Cliff asked.

"I'm not sure," Joanne said. "For a minute I thought I saw yellow smoke in the back, but it's gone now. Do you think something's wrong with your car?"

"No, the car seems fine. Are you coming back in, Cindy?" Cliff asked. "Or do you want us to leave without you?"

"Uh . . ." Cindy looked in the back seat. As Joanne had said, the strange smoke had vanished. "I . . . uh . . ."

"We're in a hurry, Cindy!" Cliff reminded her.

Cindy didn't want to abandon her friends, even though she was so scared. Finally, she got back into the car squeezing herself into the front seat next to Joanne.

A mile farther on, they heard a hissing sound behind them. The girls froze, unable to turn around to look. Cliff, however, glanced at the rearview mirror, then promptly stepped on the gas pedal.

"What is it?" Joanne asked.

"Only another mile or two," he said, hedging.

Joanne braced herself and turned around in her

seat. A fat black spider was crawling on the seat. It paused when it realized she was watching.

Maybe this was her chance! she thought, as she pulled a shoe off her foot.

"Jo, what in the world are you doing?" Cindy demanded.

Joanne didn't have time to explain. Gripping the shoe with her hand, she slammed it down on the spider.

"Jo!" Cindy cried in shock and disbelief.

There! I killed it! Joanne thought exultantly. How stupid of the vampire to change into a bug!

But the feeling of triumph was short-lived. When Joanne lifted the shoe, a puff of yellow smoke escaped. No remains of the spider could be seen.

Frantically, she looked around for the insect. It was gone, but the smoky tendril was now floating lazily in the air, changing into various shapes. It became a thin stream, a swirling spiral, then an amorphous blob with a vague face.

Joanne glanced at Cindy and Cliff. They were staring intently at the road, deliberately blocking out the scene behind them.

"Hurry," she urged Cliff.

"You told me not to before."

"I know, but hurry now."

Mist swirled in front of the car now. It hadn't been foggy earlier. Before their very eyes the mist seemed to grow appendages and transform into an animal.

Joanne wanted to shout at Cliff to stop the car,

but she couldn't find her voice. To her horror, the vaporous animal materialized into what looked like a snarling, golden-eyed wolf.

"Cliff, stop the—"

The wolf emitted a deep, guttural growl, then leaped forward to attack.

Chapter Seventeen

Joanne didn't know where she was. Her head hurt and her vision was cloudy. From a dim light on the wall behind her she could see she was in bed, in a small, unfamiliar room. Then, in a rush of alarm, it hit her. She was in a hospital!

She tried to sit up, only to find that the pain in her head was much worse than she'd first thought. What had happened? How long had she been in here?

She looked around the room. There was another bed next to hers, but it was empty.

"Well, hello, Miss Jenkins!" A young nurse smiled cheerfully as she came into the room. "I'm glad to see you're finally awake. How are you feeling?"

"My head hurts."

"That's to be expected. You have a nasty bump there."

Still smiling, the nurse took Joanne's pulse. She was not only young, but pretty with flaxen hair and sparkling green eyes. Maybe she's actually an angel, Joanne thought groggily.

"Where are the others?" she asked.

"The others?"

"The last thing I remember, I was with my boyfriend and best friend."

"Oh yes. The other two occupants in the car. They were treated and immediately released. The reason you're still here is because the doctor wants to keep an eye on your head injury, to make sure nothing more develops." Her smile widened as she added, "And I'm sure nothing will."

Joanne touched her forehead, then winced. What had she hit—an iron wall?

"You should have worn your safety belt," the nurse mildly scolded. "Luckily it wasn't worse."

"What happened? I don't remember much of it, only that . . ." She fell silent as a vivid image of the snarling, golden-eyed wolf flashed into her mind.

Had she actually seen it, or only imagined it? She recalled the yellowish smoke. Maybe something had been wrong with the car. And the wolf had been nothing more than an imaginary creation. Faces and objects were easy to see in smoke. She used to stare at clouds when she was little and imagine various things in them. It was nothing unusual at all . . .

"The car you were in collided with a tree," she heard the nurse say. "Your friends suffered a few bruises and scratches, but you, unfortunately, hit the windshield."

"Did they find anything else in the car?"

"What do you mean?"

"Something like . . . a dog?"

"Well, I'm afraid I can't tell you. After all, I wasn't there at the scene. You'll have to ask the police officers who were."

"What time is it now? Is there a phone I can use?"

"It's almost three o'clock in the morning. There's a phone at the nurse's station, but I don't think it'd be wise to call anyone at this hour."

"My friends, I'm sure they're still up—"

"The doctor gave them sedatives. The accident shook them up badly."

Is that why I feel so groggy, why I'm fighting to stay awake? Joanne thought.

The nurse patted Joanne's hand soothingly. "You just take it easy, Miss Jenkins, and everything will be fine."

She started to leave, then stopped in the doorway as she suddenly remembered something.

"Oh, one more thing, Miss Jenkins. We notified your parents in Hawaii. They said they'd be here to see you as quickly as they can."

Against her will, she fell into another deep sleep. Erik, as handsome and as charming as ever, was in her dreams. He gazed at her with his deep, dark eyes, and smiled at her with his gleaming teeth. Then the eyes and smile changed. The eyes burned with scarlet, feral light, and the smile tightened into a snarl. When Joanne woke up, she was cold and sweaty, and the throbbing pain in her head was much worse.

She found and pressed a button at the side of her bed, signaling for the nurse.

"Yes, dear?"

It was a different nurse this time. She was much older and darker, more motherly than angelic. Also, Joanne noticed it was no longer nighttime; daylight now brightened the room.

"May I have an aspirin for my headache? It hurts terribly."

"I'll have to check with the doctor first. He should be making his rounds shortly. Is there anything else?"

"I guess not." Joanne watched the nurse turn and head for the doorway, then she blurted out, "Nurse?"

"Yes?"

So many disturbing questions were on Joanne's mind. She needed someone to talk to.

"I . . . I just had an awful dream about a vampire," she began. "Do you know anything about vampires?"

The nurse laughed, but it was a laugh filled with amusement, not mockery. "Heavens," the woman exclaimed, "why would I know anything about vampires?"

"You don't know anything at all about them?"

"Well, only in what I've seen in old movies."

"What do you remember about them, nurse?"

"Oh, please, call me Mary. Well, it's been many, many years since I've seen such a movie. Full moon, dark castles, and bats. Quite dreadful.

I remember covering my eyes throughout most of those films."

"What usually happened to the vampires in them?" Joanne asked, trying to sound casual, lest the nurse become wary and start running for a psychiatrist.

"My, your dream must have been quite frightful for you to ask such questions. I certainly hope you're not carrying any notion about vampires actually existing, dear."

"No, of course not. I'm just curious about . . . the folklore."

"Well, I'm not too familiar with ancient stories and legends, but in the movies the vampire would usually be difficult to kill. Sometimes he'd die in the end, but of course not until he had claimed a few victims first."

"How did he usually die?" Joanne asked, her heart racing with hope.

"My, my, you really are a curious one, aren't you? Well, let me think. I believe there were several ways to get rid of a vampire in those old movies. One was by exposing him to sunlight. Another was to burn him in his coffin. Oh yes, and to drive a stake through his heart while he was sleeping."

"A stake?"

"Yes. I believe it has to be wooden. I can remember those scenes quite well, now that I'm thinking about it. Quite grisly, they were. Blood would splatter everywhere as the hero pounded the stake deep into the vampire's chest. I used to squirm and shiver every time that happened."

"And then what?"

"The vampire would either turn to ashes, or turn into something beastly—like the devil himself, perhaps—and die."

"Was there anything else they used to kill them?'

"Well, let me see. Garlic was used. And sometimes holy things, like blessed water or a crucifix. But I think those things would only deter the vampire, not kill him."

Joanne became silent. The nurse watched her for a moment, then said, "Oh dear, I frightened you, didn't I?"

"No, no. Of course not. You were only talking about old movies."

"That's right. It was all make-believe—and so was the vampire in your dream. I guess I shouldn't have been so explicit. People always say I babble so. They say I never know when to shut my—"

She stopped in mid-sentence as a middle-aged couple entered the room.

"Mom! Dad!" Joanne exclaimed. She was delighted, yet disappointed, to see her parents.

"Darling, are you all right?" her mother cried, rushing toward the bed.

"We tried to get here sooner, sweetheart," her father said, "but the first flight was full."

The nurse stepped aside to let the parents come closer, then quietly left the room.

"What on earth happened?" Joanne's mother asked anxiously, her attention on Joanne.

"Take it easy, Mom. I'm all right now."

"But what happened? The doctor said you'd

been in some kind of accident. I was too shook up to hear details."

"It was a car accident. I was with Cindy and Cliff. They're both okay, from what I've heard. Have you seen them?"

"We just flew in," her father said.

"We came straight here," her mother added. "I suppose Cliff was speeding and lost control of the car. Is that what happened?"

Joanne wasn't sure, although she remembered they'd been in a hurry to reach the police station.

"Well, was he?" her mother demanded.

"Clara, take it easy," Joanne's father urged his wife. "Can't you see you're upsetting her?"

"You're right. I'm so sorry. We'll talk about it later." With an apologetic smile, Clara leaned forward and kissed Joanne's cheek. "I'm so grateful that you're okay, sweetheart."

"I feel just awful for ruining your vacation," Joanne said, tears coming to her eyes.

"Don't you worry about it," her father told her. "We can always take another vacation. The important thing now is that you get better. How are you feeling?"

"Not too bad. I've a few bumps and a headache." She yawned, then added, "Sleepy."

"Is there anything you'd like for us to get you?" her mother asked. "A book, perhaps? A magazine?"

Joanne shook her head. "When will I be going home?"

"We'll have to ask the doctor."

Joanne's father left the room to look for the

physician. When he returned, it was with disappointing news.

"I'm afraid Doctor Rosewood wants you to stay one more night," he said. "He says he wants to be certain you don't have a concussion. It's just a precautionary measure, nothing to be alarmed about."

Joanne barely heard him. Already her eyelids were beginning to droop.

"We'll leave you alone now," her mother said softly, planting another kiss on her cheek.

Then Joanne felt a kiss on her forehead, and knew it was her father's.

"We'll be back," he said.

"I'm . . . sorry . . . for spoiling . . . your vacation," she said again. Her voice sounded so distant to her ears.

"Hush, sweetheart," her mother replied. "Go to sleep."

Joanne never saw or heard her mother and father leave the room. When she woke up several hours later, it was with panic.

She had forgotten to warn her parents.

Erik could still be at the house, waiting for them!

Chapter Eighteen

Joanne looked frantically at the window across the room. Darkness. She searched for a clock. None could be found. Maybe I'm panicking for nothing, she told herself. Maybe Erik had moved on. They had moved that trunk from the house.

Yet, no matter how many times she tried to convince herself of this, she couldn't stop worrying about her parents. She put on her robe and hurried out of the room to find a nurse.

"Miss, you get right back in bed!" the head nurse ordered, the instant she spotted Joanne in the corridor.

"What time is it?"

The nurse glanced at her watch. "It's a little after eleven. Now back in bed. If you need anything, just use the buzzer attached to the bed. That's what it's there for."

Under the head nurse's watchful eye, Joanne slipped back into bed. But after the nurse left, she got up again and began pacing the room. She glanced out of the window, and panic shot through her again. It was an exceptionally dark night, the stars and the moon invisible behind clouds.

She had to do something! Her parents' lives could be in danger!

In the small closet, she found her jeans, sweatshirt, and shoes, and quickly slipped into them. She made another attempt to leave her room. This time she managed to reach the elevator doors before the head nurse spotted her.

"Miss Jenkins, what do you think you're doing?"

"I have to go home. My head doesn't hurt anymore. I feel fine now."

"That's for the doctor to decide. You can go home only when he says you can."

"You don't understand, nurse. I *have* to go home—"

"I most certainly *do* understand! I have doctors' orders to follow, young lady. And that includes keeping patients in their beds. Now, you march right back to your room and don't even *think* of trying another stunt like this again!"

"But—"

"No buts! Get back in there."

"My parents could be in danger!"

The nurse eyed her suspiciously. "In what way?"

Joanne debated whether or not to tell the truth.

She knew the nurse wouldn't believe her in a million years.

"Well?" the nurse demanded impatiently.

"You might think this is crazy, but a vampire could be after them."

"A *what?*" The nurse glared at her, then shook her head, not with disbelief but with disgust. "You people will think of anything to leave this hospital, won't you? You'd think this was some kind of prison we're running here!"

"Nurse, you *have* to let me go," Joanne pleaded. "I promise I'll come right back if my parents are—"

"And make me lose my job when the doctor finds out? I'm afraid not, young lady. Now get back in your nightgown and to bed."

"Please."

The nurse pointed adamantly to Joanne's room, reminding her of a warden. This *is* a prison, she thought.

"Am I allowed one phone call?" she asked.

"No need to be sarcastic."

"I'm not," she said as she realized a phone call might help allay her fears. "If I can't see my parents, at least let me phone them."

"It's late."

"They never go to bed until after the eleven o'clock news anyway."

The nurse sighed. "The phone's on the desk."

"Thank you." Joanne dialed her home number and waited nervously as the phone rang and rang.

Were her parents sleeping already? Had they gone out? About once a week they would usually visit her Aunt Shirley and Uncle Dave. Was that where they were now?

She glanced over her shoulder, expecting to see the head nurse glaring at her. Instead, the woman was seated at the desk, reading a chart.

The phone continued to ring. And ring. At the tenth ring, the nurse finally looked up.

"Perhaps you should hang up now," she said.

"Just a few more rings, please. Just to be sure."

Wordlessly, the nurse returned her attention to the chart.

Maybe something had already happened to them, Joanne thought in a fresh rush of alarm. Maybe she was too late!

Suddenly the ringing stopped. Joanne's breath caught as she waited for someone to speak. But only silence was heard at the other end.

"Hello?" she said.

No one answered.

"Mom? Dad? . . . Who is this?"

Still there was no response. Maybe it was a bad connection. Maybe something was wrong with the phone. She started to hang up and try again when she heard soft chuckling.

"Hello?" she repeated.

"This is my lovely princess, is it not?"

Joanne almost dropped the phone. It was Erik!

"Speechless, are you?" he said. She could almost see him smirking with amusement.

"Where are my mother and father?"

He said nothing, but chuckled again.

"Where are they?" she demanded.

"It looks as if you will have to come here to find out, lovely one."

"If you did anything to them, I'll—"

The phone went dead.

Joanne stared numbly at the receiver, then at the head nurse, who was now watching her. She thought of bolting out of there, but knew she'd never make it past the lobby downstairs. Certainly, the nurse would notify someone to stop her.

"Is everything all right?" the nurse asked.

Without answering, Joanne returned to her room. She would have to think of another way to escape.

She looked out the window. It was a steep drop to the ground. She could never jump out without killing herself. Returning to the door, she waited a few minutes, then peeked out into the hallway.

Because of the late hour, not much was happening. The head nurse was at the desk, talking on the phone, her back to Joanne. The elevator doors could be seen from the desk, but farther down, almost directly across the head nurse, Joanne noticed a door marked "stairs."

If only she could reach that door without the nurse seeing her!

Another nurse appeared from the other end of the corridor, and stopped at the desk. She talked with the head nurse for a few minutes, then headed back in the direction she had come. Joanne recognized this nurse as the one she had first met, the one she'd thought was a pretty angel.

When everything was quiet again, the head nurse yawned, then pulled out a magazine to read.

Joanne waited until the woman was deeply engrossed in her reading, then slipped off her shoes and tiptoed out into the corridor. She kept close to the wall, making herself as inconspicuous as possible.

Whenever the head nurse looked up from the magazine, Joanne quickly slipped into a patient's room. To her relief, every patient she encountered was sleeping. As she neared the desk, her confidence grew. She decided that she would get to her knees and crawl quietly past the desk, and then make a dash for the stairs.

But as she thought this, the nurse yawned again and looked up from the magazine.

Panicking, Joanne rushed to the nearest door and, without looking, slipped into a room.

It was the staff kitchen, so small there was barely enough room to accommodate the stove, sink and refrigerator. Joanne could hardly move without bumping into something. In the door through which she had just entered was a tiny window.

She peeked out, expecting to see the head nurse rushing toward her, but she saw only an empty corridor. She craned her neck until she could see the desk. The nurse had resumed reading her magazine.

Joanne watched her and contemplated her next move. So much precious time was being wasted. A minute went by, then another. The nurse glanced at her watch, closed the magazine, and stood up. She looked directly at the kitchen door—at Joanne!

Had she seen her?

The nurse started toward her.

Joanne groaned. If she was caught this time, it'd be all over! The nurse would never let her out of her sight again for the rest of the night.

Frantically, Joanne looked around the room. As the door swung open, she jumped behind a metal food cart.

Leaving the door open behind her, the nurse headed straight for the coffee urn. It wasn't Joanne she wanted, it was coffee! The moment the nurse walked past the food cart, Joanne made a dash for the door.

She ran out into the corridor and headed for the stairs.

"Miss Jenkins!" the head nurse shouted, and hurried after her. Trained to respond swiftly, two more nurses appeared, seemingly out of nowhere, to converge on their quarry. But Joanne was ahead of them now. She flung open the door to the stairwell and raced down the steps.

I'm faster than any of them, she told herself. And *please* let there be no time for them to call security!

When she reached the lobby, she found it empty except for one receptionist at a circular central desk. Joanne was halfway across the lobby before the receptionist, half asleep with boredom, noticed her. By then it was too late. Joanne was out of the building.

She carefully avoided street lamps as she sped toward the highway. When she reached it, she stopped. Until now, she hadn't given transportation any thought. She could walk, but it would take at least an hour to get home.

There was no way to catch a bus or taxi. Hitching a ride seemed to be the only option, although she'd been too afraid to do this before. She reminded herself that her parents were worth the risk.

Almost instantly a car stopped. The driver was a middle-aged woman dressed in a waitress uniform. "Where're ya heading, honey?" she asked.

Joanne hesitated, then entered the car. She gave the woman her home address.

"Isn't it past your bedtime?" said the woman.

"I—I guess."

The woman studied her in silence for a moment, then concentrated on her driving.

"Y'know, I've got a daughter about your age. If I ever caught her hitchhiking, I'd ground her for a month. No, maybe a year." When Joanne said nothing, she added, "Hitchhiking is dangerous, in case you didn't know, honey. *I* could be dangerous. I could be carrying a weapon, y'know. Ever thought of that?"

Suddenly cold, Joanne began to shiver.

"Are you a runaway?" the woman demanded. "Is that it? Are ya running away from home?"

"No. I'm going home now."

"Is that so? What if I decide not to take you there, eh?"

"Please, don't do that." Nervously, Joanne looked out the window. The car was moving too fast. She was completely at the driver's mercy.

"Maybe I should take you to my place

instead,'' the woman threatened. ''I could kidnap you, make myself a lot of money from your parents. Or maybe I could be carrying a gun. I could easily shoot you and rob you. How would you like that?''

Without warning, Joanne began to cry.

''Hey, what's the matter?'' the woman behind the wheel looked at her in surprise. The hard edge in her voice was suddenly gone.

Joanne sniffed back her tears and fought to regain her composure. ''Nothing,'' she mumbled. ''It's a long story, and you wouldn't believe me anyway.''

The woman looked away and said nothing more. They drove in silence, then to Joanne's relief, her street came into view.

''The third house on the right is mine,'' she said, leaning forward in her seat.

The car braked in front of the house. The living room window was ablaze with light and the family car was in the driveway.

''Thank you,'' Joanne said gratefully to the woman next to her. ''Thank you so much!''

''Hey, listen, kid. I think I know why you were crying back there. It's because I scared you, right? Well, I'm sorry. But you got to understand I did it because I wanted you to understand how dangerous hitchhiking could be. I wasn't kidding when I said I could've been somebody dangerous, you know. I don't know if you've been listening to the news lately, but there's a maniac loose. He escaped from the state hospital and the cops haven't found him yet. They think maybe he already killed somebody not too far from here. The reason I picked you up in the first place was so that nobody else—nobody like him—could come along after me and pick you up. I care because, like I said, I got a daughter of my own. I hope by scaring you I taught you something tonight."

"You did. And again, thanks." Joanne pushed down on the door handle.

"Promise me you won't do a foolish thing like this again. Promise me you'll take a cab or bus, the next time you need a ride."

"I promise."

"Good. Now get on home."

Chapter Nineteen

The living room was empty.

"Dad? Mom?" Joanne called in a strained voice.

The television set was on. A talk show host was interviewing a famous comedian.

Joanne looked up the stairs that led to the bedrooms. Had her parents gone to bed and forgot to turn off the lights and the television set?

Please, let that be it.

As she started up the stairs, she heard a noise in the kitchen. Instantly, she froze. Was that her parents? Or was it . . .

Her father emerged from the kitchen.

"Dad!" she cried, flooded with relief. She ran into his arms, startling him. "Oh, Dad!"

"What on earth are you doing here?"

"Where's Mom?" she asked, ignoring the

question. "Is she all right? He didn't get her, did he?"

"Your mother is upstairs in bed. What are you talking about? Did who get her?"

"Mom!" Joanne shouted in alarm, then bolted for the stairs.

Her father grabbed her arm, stopping her. "You're supposed to be at the hospital. Why are you home?"

Before Joanne could answer, her mother appeared at the top of the stairs, tightening the sash around her robe.

"What's going on?" she demanded, then spotted Joanne. "What are you doing here?'

"Oh, I'm so glad you're both all right," Joanne cried.

"All right?" the woman echoed as she glanced uncertainly at her husband. "Why shouldn't we be?"

"Mom, Dad, you both could have been in real danger. Where were you tonight? I tried to call you from the hospital."

"We were at your Aunt Shirley's," her mother answered. "Your father and I were worried about you. We thought a visit would help us forget for a little while. We just got back a few minutes ago."

"Does the hospital know you're here?" Mr. Jenkins asked.

Joanne shook her head and explained how she had snuck out. "I had to," she finished. "When I called, he answered the phone. That means he's still in this house."

"Who answered the phone, dear?"

"Erik." When she saw that her parents were staring blankly at her, she added, "He's a stranger who's been living in this house. It's a long story, and I know you're not going to believe me, but I think . . . I think he might be a vampire."

"A *what*?" Mr. Jenkins frowned.

"I know it sounds crazy, Dad. But I'm sure a vampire was—is—in the house. We found his trunk in the attic. You don't have a wooden trunk up there, do you?"

"Well, no, not that I can recall—"

"Do you, Mom?"

"No, I don't think I do," her mother replied, her frown deepening.

"Then it has to be Erik's," Joanne was now confident. "He tried to kill us. He changes into different things—a bird, wolf, even a mist. He—"

"Hold it!" Her father's abrupt command silenced her. Then he turned to his wife and said in a low, concerned voice, "Go call the hospital, honey. I think she's on some kind of medication."

Mrs. Jenkins promptly picked up the phone.

"There's no time!" Joanne wailed. "Dad, can you make a stake?"

"Stake?"

"Yes, a wooden one. It's one way to kill a vampire. Mom, is there any garlic in the kitchen? Please put that phone down. You've got to believe me. I'm telling the truth." When it was evident her mother wasn't going to listen to her, she shouted, *"Please!"*

Startled by such desperation, Mrs. Jenkins hesitantly replaced the receiver.

Joanne then ran into the kitchen and searched the cupboards. To her disappointment she found no garlic cloves. She rushed back into the living room to ask her parents if they had a crucifix or anything holy. When they said they didn't, she grabbed the phone to call Cliff.

"Cliff? Cliff?" She knew she sounded like a person who had lost her mind, but she couldn't control herself. "Come on, Cliff! Answer!"

Cliff's mother finally replied. "Hello?"

"Is Cliff there, Mrs. Wright?"

"Oh, hello, Joanne!" Mrs. Wright said pleasantly, recognizing her voice. "You must be calling from the hospital. How are you feeling, dear?"

"Fine. I must talk to Cliff. Is he there?"

"He's sleeping at the moment. I hate to wake him up. This is the first time he's been sleeping without sedatives since that terrible accident."

"Please wake him up, Mrs. Wright. It's important."

"Well . . . I really hate to, dear. As I said, it's the first time since the accident. He really needs his rest. Now, if you'd leave a message, I'll be sure he gets it the minute he wakes up."

"Never mind." Joanne hung up, then immediately dialed Cindy's number.

"Hello?" Cindy answered on the second ring.

"It's me, Jo."

"Jo!" Cindy exclaimed, clearly delighted to hear from her. "How are you? Cliff and I went to see you in the hospital, but you were sleeping. The nurse advised us not to wake you up. She said you were doing okay, had a headache, but everything was fine and she thought you'd be out in the morning. Is that true?"

"I'm home right now."

"You are what? I thought—"

"I'll explain later. I think Erik is still in the house," she said. She explained about the conversation she'd had on the phone with him. "Do you remember anything about the car accident, Cindy?"

"A lot of it was fuzzy. Why?'

"Do you remember a wolf attacking us?"

"I don't know if it was a wolf. It was awfully confusing."

"What did happen then?"

"I thought I saw a lot of smoke, and then Cliff started losing control of the car. He was yelling that something was after him. And then before you know it, we were heading straight for a tree. I think I blacked out for a while, 'cause the next thing I knew, people were looking down at me, asking if I was all right."

"Do you know if anyone saw the wolf?"

"No. There was thick smoke all around us when the people came to help us. It was weird how they came out of nowhere so fast. Anyway, I think they just thought it was only smoke from the engine. When the three of us were carried to the ambulance, I looked back at the car."

"And?" Joanne prompted when Cindy paused.

"Well, as I said, everything about the accident

is fuzzy, but I think I saw a mist drift away from the wreck. I watched it leave the car and the crowd. It was like a big, dark cloud. The more I stared at it, the more I could see faces and shapes in it. At one point it reminded me of a huge dragon with wings, tail, and claws."

"Didn't anyone else notice this?"

"I don't think so. Everybody was too busy with us and the wreck to look up."

"Where did it go?"

"It sort of floated over the trees and drifted out of sight."

"In which direction, Cindy? Did it head toward my house?"

"Yes."

"So it definitely came back here," Joanne said. "And what about the trunk? Did anybody see it? Is it still in the car?"

"I already asked Cliff about it and he checked. It was gone. Oh, Jo, Cliff and I didn't know what to do while you were in the hospital. We were so afraid the vampire would do something to us or you, but he never showed. We would've looked for him again at your house, but the police had locked it up. They made us tell them where your parents were so they could notify them."

"Come on over now," Joanne begged. "And don't forget to bring garlic."

"Garlic?"

"Yes. Don't ask me why, but according to legends and old movies, vampires hate garlic."

"That's silly!"

"I know, but we must try everything. If you

can find a crucifix or anything blessed or holy, bring that too. Oh, and try to get Cliff to come with you. I tried already, but his mother wouldn't wake him up."

When Joanne hung up, she was surprised to find her parents gone.

Chapter Twenty

Joanne's father quietly closed the door to the master bedroom, then looked over at his wife.

"Is she going to be all right?" Mrs. Jenkins asked worriedly.

"I'm going to call the hospital right now," he said as he headed straight for the telephone on the night table.

"What did she mean about a wooden stake and garlic and vampire? Do you think she could be suffering from some kind of mental disorder? Do you think the car accident has done something to her head, has caused permanent damage?" Her voice rose with each question, on the verge of hysteria.

Mr. Jenkins dropped the phone to hold her tightly in his arms.

"Relax, Clara," he urged softly. "Everything's

going to be all right.'' He planted a gentle kiss on her forehead. ''Relax.''

''I can't help it. I'm so worried about her. I knew we shouldn't have taken that vacation. If we hadn't, none of this would've happened.''

''As I said before, I think it's the medication she's on that's making her behave strangely. Now if you'll calm down, I'll call the hospital and get to the bottom of this.''

Mrs. Jenkins sniffed back the tears that had rushed to her eyes and sat stiffly on the edge of the bed.

Mr. Jenkins reached for the phone once more. As he dialed, he became aware of a change in the room. He wasn't sure what it was, but he was confident he wasn't mistaken. He looked over at his wife. She, too, seemed aware of the change, for her eyes were nervously flitting to every corner of the room.

''Is it me, or is it cold in here?'' she asked.

''I felt a chill, too.'' He looked in the direction of the door. The draft seemed to be coming from there. Perhaps the front entrance had been left open and cold air was traveling up the stairs, down the hall, and into the room.

''Lemore Hospital,'' a crisp voice answered in Mr. Jenkins's ear, pulling his attention back to the phone. ''May I help you?''

''Uh, yes.'' Mr. Jenkins cleared his throat. ''I'm calling about my daughter, Joanne Jenkins. It seems she had taken it upon herself to leave your hospital and is now here with us. We're very concerned. I believe she's still under medication and—" A sharp electrical crackle exploded in his ear. Startled, he pulled his head away from the phone.

"What's wrong, George?" His wife was quickly beside him.

But he scarcely heard her. "Hello? Hello?" He shook the receiver, then shouted into it again. "Hello? Is anybody there?" Puzzled and indignant, he looked at his wife. "I think the hospital actually hung up on me!"

"Maybe something's wrong with the phone, dear. Try again."

Nodding, Mr. Jenkins called the hospital once more. The same voice answered, "Lemore Hospital."

"We were just cut off," Mr. Jenkins said. "I was calling about my daughter—"

Another crackle of static jolted him. And again the phone fell silent. "You're right. Something's wrong with this extension. Let's go back downstairs and use the phone there."

When they reached the bedroom door, it wouldn't open.

"Now something's wrong with the door!"

"Now, now, George," his wife soothed. "There's no need to get excited. Remember your blood pressure."

He twisted at the doorknob, pulled at it, and still the door wouldn't give. "I don't believe it! The damn thing is jammed! It was fine when we left for vacation."

"Now, now. Easy, easy. Your face is getting all red."

He sighed and forced himself to take heed. He closed his eyes, willed himself to be calm, and then tried the door again.

It still wouldn't open.

Joanne pushed aside the curtain and looked out the living room window. Cindy wasn't here yet. It had been over ten minutes since she'd called her, and she only lived five minutes away. What was taking her so long?

Joanne started pacing the room. Cindy'll be here in another minute, she told herself. And then, after Joanne's parents hear Cindy tell about the vampire, they'll start to believe. Joanne had thought of barging into her parents' bedroom, where she could hear them murmuring indistinctly about something, and trying to stop them from calling the hospital again, but she knew she'd be wasting her time. She would just have to wait for Cindy to arrive. Together they would help her parents.

She looked out the window again. At last she saw a car pull up into the driveway. Because it was dark outside and the headlights were blinding, she couldn't see the car too well. Nevertheless, she ran to the front door and flung it open. To her surprise she found not one, but two figures hurrying up the walk.

"Cliff!" she exclaimed.

In reply he hugged her. He was so glad to see her, so glad that she was all right.

"It wasn't easy, but I reached him," Cindy said beside them. "I told his mother that it was an emergency, a life-and-death situation, and that there was no time to go into details. I told her that she *must* wake him up, and I guess because of your phone call plus mine, she decided to believe me."

"I tried to get here as fast as I could," Cliff said. "How're you doing? I worry so much about you, Jo."

"I'm okay," Joanne told him. "It's my parents I'm worried about. Did you bring the stuff we might need?" she asked Cindy.

Cindy shook a bulky brown bag for her to see. "It's all in here."

"Good. Maybe we can scare him out of this place for good."

Back in the living room, Joanne took the bag from Cindy and emptied its contents—four cloves of garlic and two crucifixes. One crucifix was a delicate jewelry piece on a silver chain, and the other a pastel blue plastic ornament meant to adorn a bedroom wall. It seemed so unlikely that these inanimate items could actually frighten or ward off a being so powerful, so evil, as Erik.

"It was all I could find," Cindy said, sensing Joanne's uncertainty.

"I suppose it's better than nothing."

"If I had more time, I'd make a wooden stake. Dad has some lumber in the cellar I could use."

"That's only good when the monster's sleeping," Joanne reminded her. "Right now Erik is awake and somewhere in this house."

"I'd be more comfortable with a gun," Cliff said wistfully.

"Guns don't work on vampires," Cindy told him.

"I know, but what if this guy isn't a vampire? What if he's that crazy killer we've been hearing about on the news? Anyway," he turned to Joanne, "why are you so sure he's still here in the house?"

"I'm not, but he *was* here when I called from the hospital."

"Well, exactly what do we do now?" Cindy asked. Her eyes fearfully took in every corner of the room, as though expecting something to leap out at her.

"We hold this stuff and go look for him," Joanne said. "Maybe when he sees that we're, well, armed, he'll go away."

"Where do you think he might be?" Cliff asked. "Back in the attic?"

"I guess that's as good a place as any to begin," Joanne said.

Cindy groaned at the thought. "Do we have to go back up there?"

Without answering, Joanne gave her the silver crucifix and a clove of garlic. Then she gave two cloves to Cliff, who at first refused it, but she persisted. The plastic crucifix and the remaining clove she kept for herself.

"Well, here goes." She braced herself and led the way up the stairs.

The hallway on the second floor was surprisingly cold. Noticing this, the trio nervously exchanged glances. Although no one said anything, they all knew that Erik had either passed through this area or was still hovering close by. They could hear the voices of Mr. and Mrs. Jenkins in the master bedroom. Joanne's parents seemed to be discussing something, but their words were muffled. Since the Jenkinses didn't seem to be in any danger, the three friends passed the room and continued toward the other end of the hall.

They paused before the trapdoor that led to the attic. Again they exchanged glances, this time mutely asking each other whether or not to continue. After a few seconds, Cliff reached for the ladder in the ceiling and pulled it down. More seconds passed as the group hesitated. Finally they began the ascent, Cliff leading the way.

Darkness engulfed them. Up here the air was even colder.

Joanne held the garlic and crucifix tighter in her hands.

"We forgot the flashlight," she whispered, remembering that the light bulb up here had been smashed.

"No. I remembered to bring it," Cliff said, and at that instant, light speared the blackness.

The yellow beam swept the attic, then rested on the closet. The door was open, allowing the light to penetrate its depth.

Cliff moved closer and examined every inch of the closet's interior. "The trunk's not back up here," he said.

"Does that mean he's no longer here?" Joanne asked hopefully.

"No," Cindy said, her voice scarcely more than

a whisper. ''It only means that he's probably made himself a new hiding place. Maybe he moved the trunk into the cellar.''

The teenagers returned to the trapdoor and descended the ladder. As they walked down the hallway toward the stairs at the opposite end, Joanne stopped at the door of her parents' bedroom.

Cliff and Cindy, unaware that Joanne was no longer with them, continued along the hallway and down the stairs.

Joanne knocked gently. ''Mom? Dad?''

''Sweetheart, the door's jammed.'' Her mother answered. ''Did you do something to the door while we were away?''

''No.'' Joanne touched the doorknob on her side, then quickly withdrew her hand. The crystal knob was as cold as a ball of ice.

''Go down to the cellar and get my toolbox,'' her father called to her. ''I think you're going to have to take the door off by the hinges.''

''Okay, Dad. I'll be right back.''

''And please hurry, dear,'' her mother pleaded. ''There's a terrible draft in here.''

Chapter Twenty-one

Their steps were loud and hollow in the dark, silent basement. Cindy stayed so close to Cliff she nearly clutched the back of his shirt. When he stopped, she stopped.

"Maybe he's not down here," she said.

"We'll never know if we don't look." Cliff swung his flashlight up at the dusty beams in the ceiling, at the fieldstone walls, and into the depth of the cellar.

Gripped by fear, Cindy didn't want to follow him down into the darkness, but she didn't want to be left behind, either.

"I can't wait until this whole horrible thing is over, Jo," she said. She turned her light to her left. To her surprise, Joanne wasn't beside her. She looked to her right, and finally behind her.

"Cliff! Jo's not here!"

"I think she's still upstairs. She'll be with us in a minute. Hey, look!"

His light was fixed on the trunk!

Cindy's heart leaped to her throat. "Do you think it's the same one?"

Cliff moved closer until the entire trunk was under the yellow light. He touched it, then let his hand roam the wooden surface, as if to assure himself his eyes weren't betraying him. "Yep, it's the same one all right."

"Do you think—do you think he's in there?"

In reply, Cliff gripped the edge of the lid, paused a moment, then lifted it an inch. He looked over at Cindy. Although she couldn't see his face because of the darkness, she knew he was surprised to find it unlocked and was now awaiting her consent to open the lid completely.

"Maybe you shouldn't, Cliff. Maybe we should wait for Jo."

"Why?"

"It might be too dangerous."

"It's not going to be any less dangerous having her with us. The reason we're here in the first place is to find out if he's here. And besides, I don't think he's inside this thing now. It must lock from the inside, so the reason it's not locked now is because he's not in there to lock it."

Cindy suspected he was right, yet she braced herself. "Okay, go ahead. Open it."

He, too, steeled himself. He silently counted to three, threw back the lid and, to be on the safe side, jumped back.

Nothing sprung out at them.

They let a moment pass, just to be sure, then they both crept closer and beamed their flashlights into the trunk.

It was empty.

Joanne, running toward the cellar for the toolbox, heard him at the bottom of the stairs to the living room.

"Hello, princess."

The voice was deep, almost raspy. It was at her left, in the direction of the kitchen.

"Look at me," it prompted. "Turn around . . . look at me."

"Go away." Joanne adamantly kept her face averted.

"I will not leave until you . . . look . . . at . . . me."

There was a strange, hypnotic quality to Erik's voice. In spite of herself, Joanne found it enchanting, dreamy.

"Turn . . . around . . ."

"Go away," she repeated, "please."

"I see you are afraid. There's no need. If only you would turn—"

Slowly, hesitantly, she found herself turning to look at him.

He smiled approvingly. She averted her eyes, as though finding his handsome face too blinding, too attractive. "Why did you lock my parents in their room?"

"So that we could be alone, my dear. But let's not talk about them," he said, stepping closer to her, his gleaming white smile never wavering. "Let's talk about you, my pretty one."

"Stay back." Joanne shakily thrust the plastic cross and garlic in front of his face.

He looked at the objects in surprise, but to her disappointment, there was no hint of alarm.

"What is this?" he asked, amused.

"I—I know what you are. I know you're—you're a vampire!"

He looked at her calmly, his smile widening. "How interesting. Do you honestly think *those* puny things you hold can stop me? What a fool you are, my lovely one."

Refusing to be deterred, she thrust the cross and garlic clove at him again. He threw his head back and laughed, then defiantly took another step forward.

"You have to have faith for those things to work," he said, spreading his arms to welcome her.

"But I do have faith. I—I do!"

"Let's stop this foolishness, my princess. Drop these things and let's talk about you and me." He paused directly before her as she retreated against a wall. "Why are you still afraid of me?" he asked gently. "Don't you find me attractive? I certainly find you attractive."

"Get away from me. Please."

"Yes, you are still afraid. How silly. How needless."

He was staring intently at her, and there was something about his gaze that was mesmerizing. She tried to fight it, but he was too close to her now. The power, or whatever it was that was emanating from those eyes of his, was too strong.

"Please," she whimpered.

"You are so lovely," he whispered. "So . . . so lovely."

Vaguely, she heard something drop to the floor. It was a moment before she realized it was the plastic cross from her hand.

"Lovely . . ."

His lips touched her forehead. She gasped, for the kiss felt as hot as fire—or was it as cold as ice?

His lips now touched her left cheek. They were a bit cool, so it wasn't as shocking this time. He kissed her again, this time on the chin. Here his lips felt warmer. Did this mean she was growing accustomed to it? Growing to like it . . . to like him . . . again?

He pulled his head back to look at her, the grin on his face as wide as ever. "You still like me, don't you?"

"No." A part of her was still struggling to free herself from his hypnotic grip. Yet she found herself still rooted before him, gazing into the bottomless depths of his eyes.

"You *do* still like me. I can tell. And, princess, I like you. We like . . . each other." He kissed her lips.

Her mind protested. It pushed him away; it hit and clawed savagely at him. But not her body. She remained motionless, her back against the wall, her face upturned, her lips accepting his.

The clove of garlic in her hand fell soundlessly to the floor.

"Do not fight me," she heard him say. "Let yourself drift . . . drift."

She closed her eyes and began to sway. His hands clutched her upper arms to steady her.

"Drift . . ."

Her mind obeyed him, and soon she found herself floating, going nowhere, just floating. She knew she no longer had any control, that she was completely at his mercy, but it didn't matter anymore. She liked this airy sensation. She wished it would last forever.

As Erik held her tighter, she began to experience a strange closeness toward him. She now wanted to know everything there was to know about this handsome young man.

"Where did you come from?" she asked. "Why did you come here? How long will you stay?"

Answers came to her, although she wasn't certain if he had spoken or if she had somehow sensed them. "I do not like to remain in one place for very long." The words were faint whispers in her mind. "I stay until I am filled with fresh youthful blood. And then I will move on."

She listened, although she could not grasp everything. It was like listening to a song without catching the lyrics. It didn't matter, though, for the music, his voice, was lovely inside her head.

"It is much safer this way," he went on. "When one is finally aware that I exist, I am already in another place, too far away for one to find. After I am done with you, I will be gone.

"I enjoyed my stay very much. But I grow restless, and there are so many dark places in the world that I could make my temporary nest."

With those last words, he touched her neck. Was it with his lips? Or his hand?

Somewhere deep inside her, Joanne felt a twinge of alarm. She knew she should push Erik away, that he was now zeroing in for the kill. But it seemed to be such an effort to fight him.

"You have such a lovely neck, my princess," he murmured against her throat. "So fair, so delicate . . ." He gently pushed her hair back.

"Please. Please, don't."

"No need to be afraid."

She felt pressure.

Nooo!

Far away she heard voices. She did not care about them, but Erik stopped abruptly to listen. His head pivoted toward the sound. As he did this, the force that was keeping her mesmerized shattered.

Joanne blinked, feeling as if she had just awakened from a deep slumber.

"Jo! Where are you, Jo?" she heard Cliff shout.

Then she heard loud footsteps, racing toward her.

Erik looked first at her, then in the direction of the noise. He seemed to be deciding what course of action to take next.

"Over here!" Joanne's voice was weak, barely audible. She cleared her throat and called out to her friends again.

Cliff and Cindy pushed through the kitchen door, then stopped short when they spotted Erik.

"It's him!" Cindy declared, at the same instant dangling the silver crucifix in front of him.

Cliff advanced quickly with the garlic, extending his arms and exposing the cloves on his palms.

Erik laughed in their faces. "Such foolishness!"

"You've got to have faith," Joanne said, remembering Erik's words. Frantically she looked down on the floor for the items she had dropped, and retrieved them. She joined her friends, boldly brandishing the plastic cross as if it were an invincible sword.

"If you exist," she told Erik, "then I'm sure good exists as well. In fact. I'm *positive* it exists."

"Only words," Erik replied between bursts of laughter. "Only words."

"No, it's the truth. I have faith now." She clutched the cross tighter. "I have confidence. I don't think you can hurt me now." With each sentence, her determination grew. As she actually began to believe in what she was saying, she felt a wonderful sense of power burgeoning within her. "I *know* you can't hurt me."

Erik's smile was still on his face, but it now seemed somewhat forced. He glanced over at Cindy and Cliff.

"I have faith," Cliff firmly announced. "I never once doubted that good existed."

"M–me, too," Cindy added. Then, realizing she had spoken in a weak, timorous voice, she took a step forward and held the crucifix closer to Erik's face. "Me, too," she repeated with all the boldness she could muster.

Erik's smile began to waver. Joanne could see she was winning, and knowing this increased her confidence.

"Leave us alone," she commanded. "Get out of my house!"

"Yes," Cindy chimed in. "Get out."

"We're not afraid of you," Cliff declared.

The small army converged on Erik, forcing him to retreat a step at a time. His smile completely vanished. He looked uncertainly at each of the teenagers. "Keep your distance," he warned, "or I'll—"

They ignored him and moved inexorably forward. "We're not afraid," they chanted in unison. "We're not afraid."

Erik backed into a wall. The small army continued to march toward him, weapons of garlic and crucifixes at the ready. Erik lashed out at Cliff and pushed him back. Cliff responded with a violent punch to the intruder's stomach.

"We're not afraid! We're not afraid!" Cliff declared as he punched him again and again.

Joanne reached out to press the plastic cross against his exposed arm. But he shoved her backward with astonishing strength, slamming her against Cindy and knocking them both over. Someone cried out; whether it was Cindy or Erik, she wasn't sure. It had all happened too fast. But when she and Cindy were back on their feet, Erik was gone. In the spot where he had been was a bewildered Cliff, fists clenched at his sides, panting laboriously.

"What happened? Where did he go?" Joanne

asked, looking frantically around. Not a single trace of Erik could be found.

"I don't know," Cliff said as he tried to catch his breath. "I was hitting him when he . . . disappeared."

"You saw him disappear?"

"Not exactly." He sounded embarrassed.

"What do you mean, not exactly?"

"Well . . . that guy was stronger than I thought. So I went after him like a wimp after a bully—with my eyes closed. I just kept hitting him until he wasn't there anymore."

"We did it!" Cindy exclaimed. "We actually did it!"

"Do you think we destroyed him?" Cliff sounded uncertain. "Do you think he's gone for good?"

But before Joanne could answer, her parents came running down the stairs. "What on earth is all the commotion about?" her mother demanded.

"How did you get out?" Joanne asked in surprise. "I thought the door was jammed."

"It was, and then all of a sudden it wasn't. It was the strangest thing. But never mind that. What was going on down here? It sounded as if the whole house had fallen down."

Joanne and her friends exchanged glances. What did go on? Mr. and Mrs. Jenkins would never believe them. Never.

"We had a little scuffle," Joanne said at length. "But I think everything's all right now."

Chapter Twenty-two

"Now, what's all this nonsense about a vampire?" Mrs. Jenkins asked, after everyone had calmed down.

Joanne opened her mouth to explain, then changed her mind. If her parents were anything like the police, they would never believe her; they would laugh at her and her friends.

"I . . . I must've been imagining things. Being alone in the house does that, I guess."

"Oh, you poor dear!" Her mother gave her a smothering hug.

Later, alone in her bed, after she'd returned to the hospital and been officially released, Joanne began to wonder if she had actually spoken the truth. Had it all been her imagination?

Had the golden-eyed wolf she'd seen been nothing but smoke from the engine? After all, Cliff's car was an old secondhand one.

And the trunk, had it been in the closet all along, somehow escaping notice from the family?

And Erik—although he was certainly real, maybe he was nothing more than a charmer, a demented hypnotist on the loose. It seemed farfetched, but not as farfetched as his being a vampire.

But then, why had he left so abruptly when he saw sunlight that morning? Or was it something else that had caused him to flee in alarm? Perhaps it wasn't sunlight at all, but rather a noise outside the front door that she had missed hearing. After all, she'd been too charmed by him to have heard anything.

Had he almost killed her? She remembered feeling pressure against her neck. Thinking back, however, she wasn't certain if it was his mouth or hand she'd felt on her neck. Whether he was trying to bite her or strangle her, she'd never know.

And as far as the bird and cat went, she had never seen him change into any of those things, had she?

Where was Erik now? Would he ever come back?

What, exactly, had made him disappear in the end? Had it been the crucifixes and garlic? Or had he fled because he was losing his battle with Cliff, who was relentlessly punching him? And *how* had he disappeared? Out the door like most people—or into thin air? Nobody had seen him leave; it had all happened so fast.

Just then the phone rang, startling her. It was

after midnight and her parents were asleep. Quickly, she grabbed the phone so that it wouldn't ring again and awaken them.

It was Cliff. "I know it's late, but I had to call."

"That's okay. I couldn't sleep. I can't stop thinking about you-know-what."

"Erik? Well, you can relax. It's why I'm calling you."

"What are you talking about?"

"I was just lying here listening to the radio when I heard the news flash. They've finally got him, Jo! They caught the creep!"

"Who? What? I still don't know what you're talking about."

"They got the guy who escaped from the state hospital. They've found him about twenty miles from here."

"Are you sure it was him? Did the radio mention his name?"

"No. But it has to be him. He's not in your house anymore. It can't be just a coincidence. Nah, it's him all right. You can relax now."

"So you don't think it was a vampire?"

"To tell you the truth, Jo, I don't think I ever truly did. I admit I had doubts now and then, but . . . nah, I figured it had to be something logical, like this crazy guy they just caught."

"You thought something was attacking you in the car before we got into the accident," she reminded him.

"That's right, I *thought*. Our imaginations were working overtime, Jo. We were all so scared. But it's over now. They got the creep back in that hospital.

"I hope you're right."

A moment of silence passed. Cliff cleared his throat. "Jo?"

"Yes?"

"Remember when I said I loved you the other day?"

"Yes."

"Well"—he cleared his throat again—"I meant it."

Joanne's heart swelled. "I meant it too."

There was a long pause, then: "I'll see you tomorrow."

"Okay."

After she hung up, she sank back into her pillow and felt tension flow out of her. Thank God, everything was back to normal.

Smiling, she closed her eyes. Now she would be able to sleep.

But a minute later her eyes flew open as something nagged at her mind—the trunk.

Cindy and Cliff had mentioned they'd found it in the cellar. Why had it returned? Originally, she had thought it was the vampire's coffin. Now that it appeared that Erik was not a vampire, what was the trunk's actual purpose?

Was it still down there?

She closed her eyes again, determined not to think anymore about it. But the trunk would not leave her mind. At length she got up from the bed and, taking a flashlight with her, went downstairs into the cellar.

She searched thoroughly, even looked under and behind the dusty workbench. Then she went back upstairs to her room, muttering over and over to herself: "It's nothing—it's nothing." She slipped back into bed and buried herself deep under the covers. There's an easy, reasonable explanation, she told herself. But right at the moment, she just couldn't think of one, that's all.

Closing her eyes, she tried once more to fall asleep. She would only think of the good things, be grateful that Erik was finally gone, that her house was back to normal. She would think about Cliff, dream about him, plan a wonderful future with him.

But she would not give that trunk another thought. No. She would not wonder how and why it had disappeared from the cellar.

And after what seemed like an eternity, she finally fell asleep.

Spine-tingling Suspense from Avon Flare

JAY BENNETT

THE EXECUTIONER 79160-9/$2.95 US/3.50 Can

Indirectly responsible for a friend's death, Bruce is consumed by guilt—until someone is out to get *him.*

CHRISTOPHER PIKE

CHAIN LETTER 89968-X/$3.50 US/$4.25 Can

One by one, the chain letter was coming to each of them... demanding dangerous, impossible deeds. None in the group wanted to believe it—until the accidents—and the dying—started happening!

NICOLE DAVIDSON

WINTERKILL 75965-9/$2.95 US/$3.50 Can

Her family's move to rural Vermont proves dangerous for Karen Henderson as she tries to track down the killer of her friend Matt.

CRASH COURSE 75964-0/$2.95 US/$3.50 Can

A secluded cabin on the lake was a perfect place to study... or to die.

Buy these books at your local bookstore or use this coupon for ordering:

Mail to: Avon Books, Dept BP, Box 767, Rte 2, Dresden, TN 38225 B

Please send me the book(s) I have checked above.

☐ My check or money order—no cash or CODs please—for $__________ is enclosed (please add $1.50 to cover postage and handling for each book ordered—Canadian residents add 7% GST).

☐ Charge my VISA/MC Acct# ____________________ Exp Date ________

Phone No ______________ Minimum credit card order is $6.00 (please add postage and handling charge of $2.00 plus 50 cents per title after the first two books to a maximum of six dollars—Canadian residents add 7% GST). For faster service, call 1-800-762-0779. Residents of Tennessee, please call 1-800-633-1607. Prices and numbers are subject to change without notice. Please allow six to eight weeks for delivery.

Name ____

Address ______________________________________

City __________________ State/Zip __________________

YAM 0292

TERRIFYING TALES OF SPINE-TINGLING SUSPENSE

THE MAN WHO WAS POE Avi
71192-3/$3.50 US/$4.25 Can
Is the mysterious stranger really the tormented writer Edgar Allan Poe, looking to use Edmund's plight as the source of a new story—with a tragic ending?

DYING TO KNOW Jeff Hammer
76143-2/$2.95 US/$3.50 Can
When Diane Delany investigates the death of her sworn enemy, she uncovers many dark secrets and begins to wonder if she can trust anyone—even her boyfriend.

FIELD TRIP Jeff Hammer
76144-0/$2.99 US/$3.50 Can
On a weekend field trip, Tom Martin doesn't know who to turn to when students start disappearing, leaving behind only their blood-spattered beds.

ALONE IN THE HOUSE Edmund Plante
76424-5/$2.99 US/$3.50 Can
In the middle of the night Joanne wakes up all alone... almost.

ON THE DEVIL'S COURT Carl Deuker
70879-5/$2.99 US/$3.50 Can
Desperate for one perfect basketball season, Joe Faust will sacrifice anything for triumph... even his soul.

Buy these books at your local bookstore or use this coupon for ordering:

Mail to: Avon Books, Dept BP, Box 767, Rte 2, Dresden, TN 38225 B
Please send me the book(s) I have checked above.
[ ] My check or money order—no cash or CODs please—for $________ is enclosed (please add $1.50 to cover postage and handling for each book ordered—Canadian residents add 7% GST).
[ ] Charge my VISA/MC Acct# ____________ Exp Date ______
Phone No ____________ Minimum credit card order is $6.00 (please add postage and handling charge of $2.00 plus 50 cents per title after the first two books to a maximum of six dollars—Canadian residents add 7% GST). For faster service, call 1-800-762-0779. Residents of Tennessee, please call 1-800-633-1607. Prices and numbers are subject to change without notice. Please allow six to eight weeks for delivery.

Name ____________
Address ____________
City ____________ State/Zip ____________

THO 0791

NOVELS FROM AVON FLARE

CLASS PICTURES 61408-1/$2.95 US/$3.50 Can

Marilyn Sachs

Pat, always the popular one, and shy, plump Lolly have been best friends since kindergarten, through thick and thin, supporting each other during crises. But everything changes when Lolly turns into a thin, pretty blonde and Pat finds herself playing second fiddle for the first time.

BABY SISTER 70358-1/$3.50 US/$4.25 Can

Marilyn Sachs

Her sister was everything Penny could never be, until Penny found something else.

THE GROUNDING OF GROUP 6 83386-7/$3.99 US/$4.99 Can

Julian Thompson

What do parents do when they realize that their sixteen-year old son or daughter is a loser and an embarrassment to the family? Five misfits find they've been set up to disappear at exclusive Coldbrook School, but aren't about to allow themselves to be permanently "grounded."

TAKING TERRI MUELLER 79004-1/$3.50 US/$4.25 Can

Norma Fox Mazer

Was it possible to be kidnapped by your own father? Terri's father has always told her that her mother died in a car crash—but now Terri has reason to suspect differently, and she struggles to find the truth on her own.

WHEN DOES THE FUN START? 76129-7/$3.50 US/$4.25 Can

Jean Thesman

Nothing has been any fun for Teddy Gideon since she spotted Zack, the love of her life, gazing into the eyes of another girl—a beautiful girl Teddy has never seen before.

Buy these books at your local bookstore or use this coupon for ordering:

Mail to: Avon Books, Dept BP, Box 767, Rte 2, Dresden, TN 38225 B
Please send me the book(s) I have checked above.
☐ My check or money order—no cash or CODs please—for $______ is enclosed (please add $1.50 to cover postage and handling for each book ordered—Canadian residents add 7% GST).
☐ Charge my VISA/MC Acct# ______ Exp Date ______
Phone No ______ Minimum credit card order is $6.00 (please add postage and handling charge of $2.00 plus 50 cents per title after the first two books to a maximum of six dollars—Canadian residents add 7% GST). For faster service, call 1-800-762-0779. Residents of Tennessee, please call 1-800-633-1607. Prices and numbers are subject to change without notice. Please allow six to eight weeks for delivery.

Name ______

Address ______

City ______ State/Zip ______

FLB 0292

WHITLEY STRIEBER

TRANSFORMATION

70535-4/$4.95 US/$5.95 Can

COMMUNION

70388-2/$4.95 US/$5.95 Can

THE WOLFEN

70440-4/$4.50 US/$5.95 Can

THE HUNGER

70441-2/$4.99 US/$5.99 Can

THE NIGHT CHURCH

70899-X/$3.95 US/$4.95 Can

Buy these books at your local bookstore or use this coupon for ordering:

Mail to: Avon Books, Dept BP, Box 767, Rte 2, Dresden, TN 38225 B
Please send me the book(s) I have checked above.
☐ My check or money order—no cash or CODs please—for $__________ is enclosed (please add $1.50 to cover postage and handling for each book ordered—Canadian residents add 7% GST).
☐ Charge my VISA/MC Acct# ________________ Exp Date ________
Phone No __________ Minimum credit card order is $6.00 (please add postage and handling charge of $2.00 plus 50 cents per title after the first two books to a maximum of six dollars—Canadian residents add 7% GST). For faster service, call 1-800-762-0779. Residents of Tennessee, please call 1-800-633-1607. Prices and numbers are subject to change without notice. Please allow six to eight weeks for delivery.

Name ____________________

Address ____________________

City __________ State/Zip __________

STR 0991